Reilly - A Dreadful, Adorable Cat

Amber Jo Illsley

BALBOA.
PRESS

A DIVISION OF HAY HOUSE

Balboa Press books may be ordered through booksellers or by contacting:

Balboa Press
A Division of Hay House
1663 Liberty Drive
Bloomington, IN 47403
www.balboapress.com.au
1 (877) 407-4847

Printed in the United States of America.

ISBN: 978-1-4525-2696-6 (sc)
ISBN: 978-1-4525-2697-3 (e)

Balboa Press rev. date: 12/17/2014

CONTENTS

CHAPTER ONE

Be Careful Of What You Pray For

The urgent call came through one Saturday from my dear friend Lou in Nelson.

"This is an S.O.S. call. Would you do me a big favour?"

"Sure. What is it?"

"Well, you know how you've been saying how much you'd like to have another cat.... it's just that I've got a kitten here who needs a lot of tender loving care....and you said you were pretty sure you were allowed to have a cat at your new rental place..."

"That's right, I did say that and yes and I *am* allowed a cat!" I said gleefully. Pets were not allowed at the previous flat I had rented, and as I love cats, I felt quite deprived in not being able to have one. However, the landlady's Persian cat Lockie must have felt sorry for me and would pay me a visit from time to time, so at least she gave me a 'cat-fix' to keep me going!

I had been in my new rental house, formerly a pre-fabricated Electricity Board house for nearly two months when Lou's call came.

"Well, this kitten's a feisty little thing and doesn't seem to be getting on with our cats or with Tess...I thought that if anyone would be able to look after her, you would be able to."

It worked. How could I resist such words? Flattery would get a person everywhere, given the right conditions, and this was the right condition! Lou told me how the kitten had been found abandoned near Okiwi Bay, in northern South Island. They, meaning Lou and her husband Dave had seen it a week before and had tried to catch it. Since Lou's son Shane and his wife were intending to drive down to the bay to Lou's and Dave's bach the following week, Lou had asked Shane if he would keep an eye out for the kitten.

He did. There was no trouble catching the wee mite as he could barely stand up, he was so weak from hunger and exhaustion.

At first they thought he was a fluffy black kitten, but when dirt was gradually removed they discovered that he was dark grey with grey paws. As further grime was removed, the grey paws changed to white.

"Would you mind having him then?" Lou asked.

I laughed. "No, I don't mind at all."

Be careful of what you pray for.... the thought popped into my head but I dismissed it until the next day.

As Lou and Dave intended going through to Christchurch over on the east coast on the following day, we agreed on a meeting place by O'Sullivan's Bridge near Murchison, very roughly the halfway mark between Nelson and Carter's Beach, near the small coastal town of Westport. I'd had a dose of the 'flu and was still aching all over, but figured that I'd be feeling a bit better the next day and I was.

I enjoyed the one-and-a-quarter hour drive to the bridge, and was quite content to wait nearly an hour before they arrived. It gave me time to think, have a rest, and to assess the odd feelings of a new chapter of my life beginning. I wondered if I was doing the right thing in taking on another kitten when my writing work circumstances were shaky, and given that my previous cat had been so naughty and destructive. I wondered if I would be taking on more of the same! Still, being able to repay even a small part of Lou's many kindnesses over the years made it all worthwhile.

They arrived and there was a very poignant handing over of this scruffy little kitten with enormous round eyes.

"A week later and you wouldn't have been given him," Lou said bluntly. A great animal lover, even after just a week, it was pulling at her heartstrings to give up the little fellow. There were many times in the future I was to remember those words and dwell on the oft-said "if only...."

Lou's hands and arms were covered in scratches.

"Don't tell me those scratches are from kitty?" I asked suspiciously. She insisted they were from clearing gorse, but after a couple of days with Reilly, I wasn't so sure.

Lou had said over the telephone that Reilly got into a lot of mischief. Mischief or not, I was glad he did, as it proved that he had recovered. It was difficult to believe that this sturdy, chunky little kitten was nearly dead just five days before. But then, Lou is a champion of TLC and had worked wonders with the little kitten. She had occasionally said she liked animals better than humans, and there have been many occasions when I would vigorously agree with her.

I told her I had decided to name him O'Reilly, and most likely Reilly, for short.

"That's a great name," Lou said, smiling.

Reilly was so well behaved on the way home. Needless to say, the return trip was slower. I felt proud and honoured that I was to be the new Mum of this cute fluffy kitten who was doing his best to stay awake. He had not wanted to stay in the cage, and I had the feeling that he would be perfectly content to sit on a sheepswool cover on the seat next to me. He was obviously too tired to look a gift horse in the mouth, i.e. a lovely clean soft sheepswool cover to sleep upon, and his eyes started to close. He'd doze off, but then the occasional squeak of the windscreen wipers would wake him up. He'd stand for a while, his front paws on the dashboard that he could only just stretch to reach, to observe the tall trees as we drove through the Buller Gorge, then his eyes would gradually close again and sleepily he'd settle down on the soft cover again, ignoring the cage that Lou had given me. It was sitting on the floor in the passenger footwell, in case Reilly became too wakeful. Lou had also given me all sorts of kitten food and packets of treats to help him on his way in life.

A little further on in the journey home Reilly decided that he'd had enough sleep for the time being and wanted to explore the inside of my car, a Mazda RX7. Since this is decidedly distracting, I stopped the car and put Reilly into the cage. He was really too tired to protest, despite his burst of activity only moments before.

The trip finally over, I brought Reilly inside and opened up his cage. He looked around, decided the place was okay and leaped out. That evening he raced around the house, exploring, chasing his tail, his shadow - in fact, anything that moved or looked like it was about to.

What a dramatic weekend! The loss of a favourite uncle, a friend's son threatening suicide, and me, recovering from a particularly nasty dose of 'flu.

"Don't get too close," Lou had warned me when handing over Reilly.

"Don't worry," I had assured her. "I've got the same bug."

**

On the evening of Day One I was ready for bed by six o'clock. Having the 'flu and being the recipient of bad news didn't help, of course. My Uncle Cyril had passed away. I'd only recently got to know my Uncle Cyril who was a dear, sweet man, and was married to one of my dad's sisters. My dad was a very sociable man but my mother, alas, was mostly *not* a sociable person and we were not able to get to know our relatives until we were adults. But that's another story!

I'd asked my Aunty Vi about funeral arrangements and she told me that they were for immediate family only. I told her I was trying to get over a bad dose of 'flu but would have gone to the funeral otherwise. However, as I had been told, it was for immediate family members only.

"No, you look after yourself dear," she said. "We'll catch up when we get back."

"I'll come for a visit, Aunty, when you're up to having visitors," I told her. And a couple of weeks later I did so.

My uncle had had a heart attack and had passed away from a further heart attack in the ambulance on the way to Grey Hospital in Greymouth.

That was a downside of living on the West Coast; if a person was seriously ill, the local Buller Hospital was inadequate for serious cases and patients had to be transported down to Grey Hospital, roughly one and a half hours' drive away. And quite often, those patients needed further transport, across the island to the east coast - to Christchurch Public Hospital.

Reilly looked like he was all set for a long night.

"Hey you, let's party. I kinda like it here and I even think I can put up with you."

"You needn't think you're having a late night little fellow," I chided. "I'm ready for bed and you're going to bed too."

I could barely stand, I was so exhausted. Surprisingly, Reilly made no fuss about going to bed, although he somehow managed to look a little snootily at his surroundings.

"Okay, so I have my own room. While this is far better than sleeping outside in the cold and chewing on old possum skins, this is not exactly the Hilton."

"Look Reilly, everything you could possibly need during the night is here. I hope you're a good boy and don't grizzle."

"I may be only a kitten, but let me tell you, this mask covers a small face of extreme cunning and intelligence, and kittens like me do not grizzle. We infiltrate."

I closed the door; Reilly looked so small and vulnerable when I glanced back at him. My heart lurched. I went to bed. Reilly's 'infiltration' was already working.

**

When I had phoned Lou at their accommodation in Christchurch and told her that we had arrived safely and I had told her that I was holding a Poetry Society pot luck tea the next night, she was concerned for the possibility of Reilly becoming too stressed at the influx of visitors.

"I've got a strong feeling he'll be just fine," I said, adding that I would keep him in his room for as long as possible.

On the morning of Day Two I was busy with training Reilly to use the garden for a toilet, rather than the coal box! He had his own litter box but immediately decided that the coal box was more inviting. I was worried about having to spend several hours at work while leaving my new boarder at home; imagining shredded net curtains and unpleasant smells of misplaced toileting.

I needn't have worried. Reilly was sitting in his sheepswool-lined box looking innocently sleepy. I was so relieved and pleased to see him that I gave him cuddles and food. I got swiped by a small paw for my trouble.

After that it was all go with preparations to be made for that evening's pot luck tea and Poetry Society meeting - the two combined as a late house-warming party. As mentioned earlier, I had moved into that house less than two months before. And now, at party time it was fully two months later and I was still feeling the effects of the move as well as lingering 'flu symptoms. One of our members, Ted, arrived early and was immediately clawed by Reilly. Ted promptly dubbed him a little monster. He put him on the floor and as I turned to put placemats on the table, up my leg Reilly climbed. I was glad I was wearing jeans, but even so, the sharp little claws still hurt. Ted was entranced with Reilly's antics.

"O'Reilly - what a neat name for a cat," he said enthusiastically. "And boy it suits him."

What did that mean? Are all O'Reillys biters, growlers, climbers of legs - jeaned or unjeaned? Maybe they are and I just haven't heard about them. Until now, that is.

When Lou had rung me the previous week to ask me if I'd do her a big favour in taking this dear little kitten, and after telling me all about him, I said he couldn't be any worse than Honeybelle. Honeybelle of Mandalay was the rather grandiose name I'd given a fine healthy ginger female kitten, in the hope that after her initial bad behaviour, she would improve. She didn't. She got worse, but how I had envied her supreme energy and assertiveness! I did not, of course, approve of her tearing the feathers off my Operatic

Society hat, and growling at me for my attempt to remove the feathers from her mouth; nor did I approve of her terrorizing my tortoiseshell cat Muffy and my visitors. She did, however, make Pet of the Week in the New Zealand Woman's Weekly.

Anyway, the saga of Honeybelle of Mandalay is yet another story. I just hoped Reilly wasn't as bad as she. No cat could be, I thought - not even as bad as New Zealander Murray Ball's cat Horse, portrayed in his internationally-acclaimed comic strips.

But all that was before I came to know Reilly...

During the course of the evening Reilly grizzled and scratched at his bedroom door. We were having fun and he wasn't. I decided that now was a strategic time in which to introduce Reilly to the rest of the Society members - at least I *thought* it was a strategic time! Reilly looked so sweet and fluffy nestled in my hands; then he went into action. Up and down legs and arms he went. For the first of his two encores he looked beseechingly up at big Mike with the deep voice. Mike was sitting down with his long legs straight out, at a perfect leaping height for Reilly.

"You're a lovely little fellow, aren't you?" Mike said softly.

Reilly leaped up, sunk his claws into Mike's leg and swung, claws firmly embedded.

"Ouch! You little bastard!"

I almost felt the pain myself. Mike was fascinated, nevertheless. Reilly's second act for an encore was to upend my lovely begonia and look at us disgustedly.

"Okay, okay, it wasn't my fault! You shouldn't have had it sitting there!"

I sympathized with my poor plant which had been flourishing beautifully until Reilly came to stay.

"I'm a kitten and therefore adorable. Plants are definitely well down on my list of priorities."

Reilly looked at me, his masked face both innocent and beguiling. I wasn't fooled. Having had a great deal of experience with cats in the past, I had come to know that look very well.

Dot, another Poetry Society member, was disappointed when I put Reilly to bed.

"What made you name him Reilly?" she asked.

"It's short for O'Reilly and it seemed to suit him."

"It does too," she agreed.

I ignored Reilly's plaintive meows and thumps on the varnished bedroom floor. I reminded myself that this was, after all, only the second day and my life - although seldom boring - was rapidly being turned upside down. Did I mind? I'm not sure. It certainly beat the feeling of loneliness that most people experience when living alone, and working mainly from home. Reilly's arrival also meant a lot more work!

The voice came unbidden. *Remember what you prayed for.*

I smiled in memory. I had prayed for a big tough tomcat to keep the numerous wandering dogs off my section. Part of the problem was that the fences were little more than a short excuse for fences, they were that low, and neighbouring dogs simply stepped over them to come wandering into my rented property. Apart from that, the driveway was open - although there was a rather rickety gate there which I didn't bother to pull across the driveway as it was the same ridiculous low height at the fencing.

A tough little kitten? I had prayed specifically for a big tough tomcat, I argued.

Do you not think the kitten will grow? came the straightforward answer.

Of course! I had temporarily forgotten that our prayers aren't necessarily answered the way we think that they should be answered!

**

CHAPTER TWO

Meeting the Neighbour

On Day Three, Reilly met Pepsi, the next-door neighbour's neat, compact grey coated, green-eyed cat. They hissed at each other and I dangerously kept my hand between them. I knew what a strong cat Pepsi was, and not averse to swiping me.

She meowed and rubbed against my legs.

"Hey listen, I don't mind *you* at all. But where did you get this scruffy little excuse for a cat from?"

"Don't refer to me as scruffy, O Grey One. I may be little, but boy am I tough and you'll find out just how tough in due course!"

"Hiss, hiss spit!"

"Spit!"

"Now now, you two. You've got to learn to be neighbourly," I said. "Pepsi, this is O'Reilly."

"O'Reilly? What sort of a name is *that?*"

"Look buster, it's *my* name and it's a tough cat's name, so just watch it."

"Pipsqueak."

"Good things come in small parcels, and I don't mind using a cliche."

"Hiss. *You* should have been introduced to *me*, not the other way round. Humans slip up all the time."

"Hiss yourself. They can't help it. They're born that way."

Pepsi growled and hissed again. Reilly, in a sudden frenzy of playfulness danced towards Pepsi and was treated to another hiss, a furious spit and a wallop across his face. Reilly looked taken aback when Pepsi, immediately following the assault, ran away and leaped the fence.

"A hit and run, that's what I call it!"

"Oh you poor little kitten! That was mean of Pepsi but never mind. She's only jealous; you've taken over part of her territory, that's why."

Reilly seemed unconcerned, promptly showing me how well he could go to the toilet in the garden, and how well he could scratch the sandy soil over the path.

The day was not yet done. I wished I hadn't just thought that. Reilly was at his worst so far, chewing the name tag off my favourite plant Ben, an excaecaria bicolor. Not satisfied with chewing up the name tag, the soil had to be aerated as well - and airborne! I seemed to be constantly picking up the hearth brush and broom that day.

Bathtime: I picked up Reilly and showed him the running water.

"No Reilly, that's for me - there's no need to look so alarmed."

"Phew! I thought for a moment you were going to put me in that hell-hole."

I got in the bath and vanished from Reilly's sight. He cried; he could hear the noise of the water but couldn't see me. I poked my head, wrapped in a shower cap, over the side of the bath. Reilly hissed and leaped back.

"I just *knew* there was a monster in there!"

"It's me, Reilly," I said, and watched his fur settle back down. I lay back in the bath. He howled so I lifted him by his scruff to the corner of the bath so he could see what was going on. He was not impressed.

And nor was I, with the red claw marks over my legs and concentrated around my knees. The hot water caused the scratches and bites to sting. With having Reilly in the house for just two days plus a few hours, already it looked like I'd been through a war zone.

I jotted down a reminder to my friends. *If you want to visit me, wear heavy jeans, boots, thick jacket and gloves. Never mind the fact you might expire from the heat; it's far better than being used for a scratching and climbing post.*

At this point in writing the first draft, my leg was smarting from scratches Reilly delivered while leaping from one chair to another and missing the chair - but not my leg.

On that particular day I was going to write an article for a South Island-wide newspaper. First of all I had book festival correspondence to deal with and then I intended beginning my story. Not a chance. Reilly had other ideas. He wanted - no, *demanded* attention, and when it wasn't immediately forthcoming he jumped onto my lap and crackled loudly his delightful kitten purr.

It never fails. That delightful crackling before the deeper tones have gradually developed is guaranteed to melt the sternest heart. Mine had been feeling pretty stern by then. My sore knees and stinging hands were a sharp reminder.

P.G. Wodehouse once said that the trouble with cats is that they've got no tact. How right he was! It is not tactful to sit on one's manuscript while trying to write, nor is it tactful to sit on the newspaper while attempting to read - or all those other pleasures in life one normally expects to undertake with a minimum of difficulty.

As I write this, Reilly is perched half on my right shoulder and is supported by my left hand. Not an easy position to be in I assure you, but it's more tactful for Reilly to be there than sitting on my first draft and attacking my pen.

"Did I promise you a bed of roses? No I did not. And there you have another cliché, and don't forget I'm only a dear little fluffy kitten."

"Oh Reilly, you're such a cunning little thing," I said, warming to him afresh.

Reilly discovered a newspaper - one I was reading. It was so much more fun than any other boring old newspaper. By the time

I'd finished reading, it was well and truly dismembered. And so his love of tearing up paper was well and truly established.

**

Reilly lay in my arms. I was suffering from 'flu still and couldn't reach for my handkerchief. I sniffed loudly. Reilly leaped from my arms with fright and landed with a thud on the floor. And sat there looking bewildered.

I like to think his action had nothing whatsoever to do with my sniffling, and everything to do with the fact that he was already in a jittery mood and maybe the haunting Enya CD I was playing was enough to set him off. I shall blame the song. When the lady reached some particularly high notes Reilly skittered around, eyes wide and staring. Only a short while before I'd walked into his room while he was in there and he'd hissed and spat at me in fright.

"It's only me, Reilly," I said, amused. He came out crackling his kitten purr.

On Day Three I rang my friends Lou and Dave. I'd had the feeling they had just arrived home, and so they had. They had just begun unpacking and were wondering how Reilly was. Was he okay? *Okay?* He was more than fit - a ball of energy while *I* was the one they should have been asking after!

By Day Four my hands were a mess and thick cord pants were a *must*. Even so, the claws still sunk right through.

Pepsi hung around, curious but still angry. Cheekily, Reilly skipped sideways up to the ranchslider door and Pepsi hissed and took a swipe, the glass door fortunately between them. Reilly bounced around directly in front of the door and taunted Pepsi, who continued to stare in and hiss - but didn't run away this time. Curiosity had got the better of her.

Reilly skipped and pranced in front of the door until boredom set in. He yawned, flopped down and went to sleep. Pepsi stared down at him as if she couldn't believe he would have the audacity to go to sleep while *she* was there. Disgusted, and with an aloof air, she padded away. Reilly watched her leave with one eye half open, and I would swear he was smirking.

As the days went by he ate well and grew more rapidly than any other kitten I'd had in the past.

"Squee!" he piped plaintively. "Squee!" Which translated meant: I need attention - *now!*

I picked him up and cuddled him close: he promptly sank his claws into my neck.

A man by the name of Joseph Wood Krutch once said that cats seem to go on the principle that it never does any harm to ask for what you want.

"Squee."

Day Four completed: I looked at my hands, covered in red spots and scratches from where You Know-Who had sunk his claws. As each day went by I was becoming more and more convinced that Lou's scratches were definitely *not* from cutting gorse back on their section. My hands were very distinctly taking on the same appearance as Lou's.

Reilly sits at the back of my chair as I write this. I'm sitting on the edge. Isn't that always the way when there's a cat in the house? I'm playing the very beautiful Enya CD again and this time Reilly seems soothed by it. Which is quite a change from the previous night's antics.

**

I should have known Reilly's spell of peace and contentment was only that - a spell, and a short one at that. He was on the go again, and at the time I had my friend Jan visiting and I had invited her for dinner. Finally, so he didn't pull too many threads in Jan's trousers, I put Reilly to bed while my friend and I had our evening meal. Reilly was surprisingly well-behaved and a couple of times during the course of the evening I had to check in on him to make sure he was okay. He was, and soon after our meal was finished I fetched Reilly out from his room and he happily played with a few toys until Jan was ready to leave.

The next day a farmer friend visited, bringing a bottle of cream sherry.

"If you've got a bit of time spare Bill, why not have a wee drop of the sherry now?" I figured that since it was late enough in the day and the bottle of sherry was technically a late house warming present, my conscience was clear.

Bill said he had a few minutes spare, so why not? I got out my beautiful little sherry glasses and we had a sip. I was in a silly mood and had barely said in a posh voice "this is so civilized" and smiled, when Reilly leaped onto Bill, nearly causing him to spill his drink.

Bill embarked on one of his interesting stories of yesteryear, his stories punctuated with "ows" and "ahs!"

"Don't be too polite, Bill," I said. "If Reilly's hurting too much, put him on the floor."

By then Reilly was at the back of Bill's neck, exploring the contours, then off down his arm and onto his leg and down the side to briefly swing there. It was almost a repeat of Monday night's performance with Mike. Only this time the recipient didn't swear. Bill's face was a study however, of pain and astonishment - no doubt the latter at how such a small animal could be so *bad*.

Another friend arrived while Bill was still there and Reilly promptly leaped onto his lap then crawled up under his armpit and swung from his thick jumper.

"Hey, this beats climbing trees any day, and I like the taste."

There is no accounting for taste, however. I can only conclude that since it was obvious that the visitor did not use a deodorant - it was no doubt salt from the man's perspiration that Reilly was after.

"Reilly, get down from there!" I said sternly. He ignored me of course. Why I bothered to open my mouth, I really do not know.

That friend didn't return to my house for some weeks – I can't think why!

Bill had left a few minutes after the next friend, Frank had arrived, and on leaving, Bill said "at least he's leaving *me* alone! That's one tough little kitten you have there!"

I was beginning to think my home was more like a railway station, there seemed to be that many people arriving and then leaving...hastened on their way by Reilly, of that I am convinced, but at least Frank was expected. We were heading down to Greymouth on Arts Council business. In the meantime my phone kept ringing, and I was glad when we were able to head away.

Later on in the day I returned from that trip to the official opening of the Greymouth Arts Centre. The Governor General at the time Sir Paul Reeves was going to be there and my friend Frank and I, as representatives of our local Community Arts Council were looking forward to meeting him. Unfortunately he was not able to be present and a letter of apology was read by the chairperson. Still, the official opening went off extremely well despite Sir Paul Reeves' absence and the bitterly cold day.

Afterwards, cups of tea and food were offered, while a local band played. I couldn't help wondering what Reilly was up to, but made a determined effort to put him out of my mind for a while.

Back home, I felt quite satisfied with the day. Reilly had been very good and had obviously slept all afternoon. But his renewed energy left me drained. He swung off my hands and arms; climbed up my leg when I was talking over the telephone, and leaped onto the top of the fridge, knocking over my fern and Easter and 'Welcome To Your New Home' cards. My Avon catalogue was next to go. In twenty seconds flat it was a ruinous mess. The Avon lady would be horrified, I thought.

Reilly eyed me defiantly.

"You did say it was a cat-a-logue. That's a log for cats, so it's mine and I can do what I like with it, so there. And I'm ripping at it, see?"

"Oh are you?" I said sarcastically. "I hadn't noticed."

"I hope you notice now, woman."

"How did you get to become so smart at such a young age?"

"Street-wise, baby."

"Don't you smart-talk me, cat! Out you go to cool off!"

And off he went, dancing in my garden, spreading more sand over the footpath and chewing the plants. Pepsi came over to investigate.

"Hey you! Remember, I may be small but I am tough."

"You don't frighten me, pipsqueak."

Reilly's head bobbed down; his little round bottom wriggled and he took a flying leap towards Pepsi who hissed and ran away.

"Da bigger dey are, da harder dey fall!"

"Someone should teach you a lesson before you're much bigger, pipsqueak."

"I notice you're saying that now you're on the other side of the fence!"

"Yawn. I can't be bothered with you. Go away."

Reilly danced up towards the fence. Pepsi was on the other side, peering through the slats.

"Hiss, spit! Keep on *your* side, buster!"

"I'm gonna take over all dis territory."

"Hiss."

"Hiss, spit!"

Reilly's fur was up, back arched, masked face amusing in this light. I had a little chuckle to myself. Two gentle dogs belonging to the neighbours further over in the other part of Martin Place wandered onto Pepsi's patch. She ignored them. Reilly - fat little Reilly - managed to squeeze between the slats and did a little dance in front of the dogs. How cheeky but how cute he looked! On Pepsi's patch an' all. The dogs ran away. I felt desperately sorry for them. But hadn't I wanted a tough cat anyway? Hadn't I been tired of all the doggy doings I'd had to clean up? And when the doings were finally espied, there was not a dog in sight to claim ownership!

After Reilly had moved in there was no further problem with doggy doings on my lawn. I could imagine the gossip in the animal population in this little neighbourhood.

"Hey, have you seen the tough kitten who's just moved in on the corner?"

"Yeah, a real smart guy, but don't ask me to take him on."

"I think he's a she. But I could be wrong."

"Even worse. They're more cunning and have wicked tongues."

"Well it's a cat, after all. What else can you expect?"

"I dunno. But if you decide to go visiting, leave me out of it, okay?"

"Uh-huh. I might not go myself."

"Could be a wise move. What say we play it cool and just observe proceedings?"

"Yeah. I'm all for playing it safe."

**

REILLY — ACE OF CATS !?

CHAPTER THREE

Growing Pains

There was a loud thump. I turned to see what mischief Reilly had got himself into this time. He'd managed to leap onto the bench - to steal the dilapidated sponge/pot scourer and proceed to try to eat it. Lord knows why. Then again, I thought, why not? After all, he'd sunk his teeth into just about everything else in the house.

I retrieved the pot scourer and threw it into the sink.

"Oh well, I didn't like the taste much anyway. Give me decent cat food any day. Hey! I'm a poet! I could sit in a tree and read poems. That would make me a poet tree cat, or *poetry* cat!"

He sat on a chair and nonchalantly washed his paws.

I glanced at those enormous paws, already average adult size, and Reilly at only around nine weeks old. I put his birthday at approximately March 17, and then I thought about the date. Of course! No wonder I'd had an overwhelming urge to name him O'Reilly, March 17 being St Patrick's Day and the day my mother made sure she was wearing green clothing and hung her washing out with green pegs.

I made vague plans for Reilly's first birthday celebration next St Patrick's Day. I wondered if he would appreciate green milk and green food. No, probably not, I decided. Maybe just a pretty green bow and new green toys would be sufficient.

He thundered around the lounge and leaped onto the drying bits of branches I'd brought inside to use as kindling wood, left over from a couple of trees cut down next to my carport. Reilly enjoyed the rustling of the tinder dry leaves, and I imagined the mess I'd have to clean up shortly. Oh well, I kept reminding myself, at least he's healthy and happy.

I watched him attack the Avon catalogue again, flitting around in mid-air to attack it from another angle. The small book is well named, I thought. Trust Reilly to see it as a cat-a-log.

Reilly's bottom looked fluffy and enormous as he pounced. With a pang of regret I thought - *he's growing so quickly and I've only had him six days*. Was it only regret that I felt? Or was there some other emotion as well? Maybe it was regret at how my life had been disrupted, and how *battle scarred* I'd become in such a short time.

I still hadn't been able to finish my article for the newspaper; when I had peace enough in which to write it, I was too tired, and when I wasn't too tired, Reilly wouldn't leave me alone. I knew I had a deadline to meet, and had to adhere to it. Reilly had other plans.

"You should be pleased I pay you this much attention! As you know, we cats are normally noted for our aloofness."

In another frenzy of activity he leaped onto my lap, his claws pinpricks of pain, and began chewing at the buttons on my overshirt. It is most disturbing trying to write while a fat kitten is determined to remove one's buttons. I shook my car keys at him; he shot away, claws sinking for leverage into me. By now I was beginning to get used to the pain. Reilly thought that my shaking the keys at him was some sort of game, and that I was about to chase him but no, I carried on writing.

"Look, the night is young and I need entertainment!"

I was really, truly tired. It had been an enjoyable, but long day, with many phone calls and visitors even before Frank and I had left for Greymouth. I wanted to go to bed for a relaxing read, but Reilly insisted I stay up for a while longer. It didn't matter to him that I was yawning and bumble-footed. Dear me no. A cat (or kitten) does not want you to think it might be compassionate; to a cat that could suggest weakness, and weak a cat (or kitten) is *not.*

As I had said earlier on, a cat has no tact. Well, I didn't *originally* say it; that amusing fellow P.G. Wodehouse said it. And I'm reiterating it.

Come to think of it, tact or not, Reilly hadn't crackled for a day. I wondered if he thought that *I* thought he was getting too soft, and therefore to purr his crackling purr could suggest that he had a much softer, pleasant side to him, a side that he did not want me to see, for some reasons of his own. I could see life was going to get even harder as the days wore on, particularly if he intended getting tougher than he already was, and starting at such a tender age.

Drawing on reserves of energy I didn't know I still had, I brought my camera gear from out of my bedroom and set my camera up ready for action. Reilly was most interested. I had to keep throwing him toys and bits of screwed up paper for his distraction. The camera and swinging shoulder strap were new and different and therefore warranted closer inspection. I managed to take what I hoped were some good shots: Reilly playing cutie-pie on the sofa, Reilly playing with leaves on small dry branches; Reilly picking his teeth with twigs, gangster-like; and Reilly with movements slowing and eyes beginning to close.

I managed to finish my story, write a caption to go with the photographs I'd taken specifically for that story and print out the story in readiness for sending away, along with the article and caption on disk. I also printed out the same story, albeit edited for other newspaper and magazine word requirements and accompanying photos. It didn't always work that way, but the more mileage I could get from one article, the better it was for me, physically and economically.

Thank goodness I could finally go to bed.

**

Several days later I telephoned Lou in Nelson, to give an update on Reilly and to ask if she could put me up for a couple of days. She said yes unhesitatingly, and asked if I intended bringing Reilly. As Nelson had suffered from a strong earthquake and her cats had been most upset by it, I thought it wiser to put Reilly in the cattery.

Although I had not personally inspected the relatively new cattery, another friend, who is secretary of the SPCA said that their Association had given it a good report: that it was clean and spacious. I rang the cattery owner and had a good chat to her.

The twenty three and a half kilometer trip to the Waimangaroa cattery was without incident. Reilly behaved perfectly and did not seem at all perturbed by being back in the car. If anything, it was a repeat of his adventure in coming to the West Coast less than two weeks before.

I had already met Lois, the cattery owner at a meeting unrelated to cats, and had thought at the first meeting that there was something special about her. Of course there is! She is another cat lover. It was nice to meet her again and make the connection to our first meeting. A former workmate had just delivered her two exotic Burmese cats to Lois, and they were yowling. Reilly stared at them with a sort of arrogant interest and then inspected his own settling-cage. It was warm and padded, with plenty of room for an active little puss. The exercise room was clean and airy, with a great view of Lois' Red Shaver hens. Reilly went into a pose of fierce concentration when he saw them.

"Too big for you, Reilly," I said.

He ignored me, as usual, and continued staring.

"You can get that idea out of your head," I said sternly.

He glanced around at me in annoyance. "Be quiet, woman! Can't you see I'm concentrating?"

I was glad I had interrupted his concentration, and then thankfully the hens moved away to safety. I had no doubts that Reilly was about to leap at one or even several of them.

All at once I felt tearful at leaving him. I gathered him up to give him a kiss, and then Lois put him into his new accommodation and locked the cage door. Reilly wasn't upset; there were too many interesting noises around, but as for me - I felt bereft. How could a little cat do that to me in less than two weeks, you may ask?

Reilly, as you will already have discovered from reading this, was no ordinary kitten. He had a huge personality, more befitting to a tough old tomcat which had seen the ways of the world and was jaded by them, but still full of adventure.

As I was in the process of turning my car around, Lois was already coming back out her door with a large container of special kitten formula milk.

I knew I'd left Reilly in capable hands. I drove away, already missing him but at the same time hoping on my return that Lois would be able to tell me whether Reilly was male or female. A girl, Lou had told me, although she added it was hard to tell "with all that fluff on her, although I usually refer to her as 'he' or 'him'." Her voice also told me she hoped I didn't mind. Mind? No, of course not, I'd said. Boy, girl, or gay - if it was a kitty in need then *I* was the answer. In any case, since I'd had Reilly, I'd referred to him as male, but on one of the few occasions I'd tried to investigate to be sure, Reilly had swiveled around and looked at me in disgust.

"How would you like *me* checking you out to see if you're a boy or girl?"

I'd put my hands on my hips and stated: "I don't *need* checking out - it's obvious I'm a female!"

Reilly had looked at me and blinked, one, two, and then three times.

"So? *I* am what I am, and do not wish to have age or sex labels attached - except when it suits me, of course. Anyway, I'm a boy kitten, so there. Maybe tomorrow I'll be something else."

"Like what?"

"A *Super* Cat!"

"Right," I'd agreed with a grin, already sure from the word go anyway, that Reilly was indeed a boy.

**

The trip to Nelson was uneventful except for there being more traffic than usual, owing to a speedway meeting being held in Westport and, I suspect, other sporting events further down the Coast at Greymouth.

It was wonderful to see Lou, her husband Dave, and their animals. Their German Shepherd/Spaniel cross Tess barked furiously when she heard the door open downstairs. I walked up the stairs and called "it's me, Tess. It's only Aunty Amber."

"Whuff."

Tess grinned and wagged her tail.

"Excuse me," I said to her as I always did when she stood in the entranceway. Tess seldom moved for me, and Lou had to ask her to move.

Lou and I chatted while she did some of chores and I rang a few people I needed to contact for additional information on the extensive school history I was compiling for a book, to be published in readiness for that school's jubilee celebration the following year. I also met up with a mutual friend of ours - John, who derided Lou and me for the fuss we made over our cats. John didn't fool us of course; we knew that despite his gruesome job as a meat inspector, he still retained a soft spot for domestic animals.

I proudly told him about my cat; full name O'Reilly.

"O'Reilly? Sounds as if he should have Seamus attached to it," John commented.

I seized on the idea. "Great!" I exclaimed. "Seamus O'Reilly it is!"

"What a mouthful."

"I'll continue to call him Reilly for short."

"That sounds more like it."

"I'll ask Reilly what he thinks of his additional name when I pick him up from the cattery when I go back."

"You talk to your cat?" John gave me an odd look.

"Of course. Doesn't everyone?"

"I suppose so."

"And Reilly talks back," I said, smiling.

"Oh yeah, sure he does," John agreed, but with a cynical look.

Ginger, Lou's large marmalade cat was not as responsive as usual. He was cuddled up in his sheepswool blanket, still recovering from shock after the earthquake, and Ninja (otherwise known as Ratty) just gazed at me from his wonderful black and white face. He promptly lowered his head back to his sheepswool rug after deciding that I was no threat. Ratty took up one armchair and Ginger half the sofa, so there wasn't a lot of seating room left for John, Lou and me.

Tess wandered in, grinning and investigating. When all proved to be homely and comfortable, she fetched her 'footie', a rugby ball-shaped yellow toy which, when chewed issued forth squeaks and squarbles.

And so our conversation was interspersed with squeaks and squarbles. It was all very relaxed and homely indeed, with added humour in watching Tess with her 'footie'. That evening, after Dave had finished working his shift in the bar downstairs and had joined us, we all enjoyed a meal at a nearby restaurant and the next day was taken up with visiting and doing interviews, concluding with watching a wonderful video on cats.

Sunday dawned crisp and sunny with a minus five degrees Celsius frost. Lou, Tess and I went for a most pleasant walk in the city. I felt very proud standing next to Tess just outside the supermarket while Lou did her shopping. People waiting in the queue stared at us, making flattering comments about Tess. I'm sure Tess knew people were talking about her but she ignored them in her regal way. She was magnificent; having been born with the best of both dog species; the size, looks and colouring of the German Shepherd and a curly back of a spaniel.

I wondered vaguely if I could train Reilly to sit like that, and if *he* would be the recipient of admiring looks. No, I decided. I had the feeling both Reilly and I would be looked upon as oddities. The vague thoughts drifted away when Lou emerged from the supermarket, resplendent in her multi-coloured knitted jacket and with her lovely long wavy ash blonde hair shining in the sunlight.

**

That afternoon I visited Cable Bay with our friend John. Cable Bay was stunning; the sea a glorious hue of green and deep blue, the sky clear and bright with a gentle but crisp breeze, and the sounds around us clear and sharp. We went for a giggling walk part way up the official walkway where the views were breathtaking. I say a giggling walk: I did most of the giggling as I kept sliding on the grassy slopes.

I wondered if Reilly would enjoy this scenery. I'm sure he would have, I immediately told myself. I was missing the little fellow badly and could hardly wait until I saw him again.

After the Cable Bay excursion, we stopped at a small tearoom on the main road and enjoyed a thick milkshake. It had been a wonderful day, beginning with the shopping jaunt, and then later a visit to a friend of Lou's who had a cat with a bad abscess. Lou gave her good, sound advice and half an hour later we were back on the road.

All up it had been a very full weekend, with more visits made on my way back down to the West Coast. I looked forward to seeing Reilly again but at the same time I felt sad at leaving Lou.

**

CHAPTER FOUR

Excess Energy

Two and three-quarter hours later I reached home. I quickly unloaded my gear and made two phone calls; to Lois at the cattery to let her know I was back in Carter's Beach and about to leave again to come and pick up Reilly, and to another friend about a meeting I thought was to be held on that night (but wasn't). Back up to Waimangaroa I went and picked up Reilly who had grown in those three days I had been away. He looked wonderfully alert.

Lois said she had thought I would want to leave picking him up until the next day.

Afterwards, I wondered why I hadn't given myself a little more time out from him.

"Well?" I said. "What *is* Reilly? A boy or girl? I personally think he's a boy, and have referred to him as a boy from day one."

Lois laughed. "I still don't know! I tried to have a look but he didn't seem to like it very much."

That was an understatement! I surreptitiously looked at Lois' arms to see if Reilly had been gouging them but Lois, sensibly, had her arms well covered with a thick jumper. I thanked her for looking after Reilly so well, paid her and left, Reilly enjoying the ride back home and being exceedingly well behaved.

But how he made up for his good behaviour! A cattery can be a good place to be, and indeed Lois' cattery was well-designed, clean and roomy but there still wasn't as much room as there was

27

at home. He went crazy: up and down furniture he sped, leaping at imaginary shadows, got spooked at slight noises, arched his back if I made a move to get up from the table, hissed and skipped sideways.

What a bundle of fluffy energy; what riotous dancing and prancing! Up on the kitchen bench to steal my dishcloth, leap down and run away with it with his head held high. What strange fascination did the dishcloth, reeking of Lux detergent, have for my little cat? I was bone weary and my neck muscles ached from the long drive. I went to the bathroom and prepared for a soak in the bath.

A strange cry came from another room. "Reilly?" I called, then came another strange, strangulated cry. It came from my bedroom. As I quickly turned to run, a muscle in my neck cramped. The pain was intense but I did my best to ignore it. "Reilly?" I called again and looked under my bed. Reilly was under the fringing at the side, his head on an odd angle. I lifted part of the bedspread up and saw what the problem was. Reilly, in his hyperactive antics, had managed to unravel one of the pieces of fringing and had his head caught in the noose he'd made for himself. It was too tight to release without causing him further stress. I grabbed my manicure set from the table by my bed and used the small scissors to snip through the noose. Reilly's choking continued and so I gently massaged his little neck and crooned over him until he recovered. Which wasn't long. Two minutes later he was biting my ankles and climbing up my leg. He was free, and determined to celebrate as quickly as possible and with as much hyperactivity as he could summon up.

My neck hurt unbearably. I massaged it hard and tried to ignore the pain of Reilly leaping up my leg. What drama - and all in the space of less than four minutes.

The massage took away the cramp, but the stinging in my leg continued.

**

I still had work to do on the school history project I had been commissioned to do. A final draft manuscript, complete with the printer's instructions written in red, is not the sort of thing you want a hyperactive kitten near. Reilly was determined to get at it, just as I was every bit as determined that he should *not*. I wanted to read through the complete manuscript again in case I found any typing errors I'd overlooked the first time round. I made a few small changes in between keeping Reilly at bay and in the end I put him to bed, and wondered why I hadn't done it earlier.

"Making a martyr of yourself, as usual," one or two of my friends would have said.

I recalled the time a short while before when I was so overloaded that the amount of work I still had to do seemed too big to overcome. I had returned home after being on call at the local newspaper, plus did an interview for my freelancing work on the way home, and knew I would have to write that evening. I came inside and went straight through to the clothesline to take my washing off the line. Back inside, I couldn't think where to put the basket of clothes. Everything suddenly seemed to be insurmountable. Jobs and articles to do loomed in front of my eyes. Suddenly I heard the words, clearly, "Lord help me to take one day at a time", from the well known country song by Cristy Lane, among other well-known singers.

I was looking at my workload in its entirety, rather than thinking about one job at a time, completing that and then moving on to the next. It was a good reminder to me to not get myself so overloaded in the future that I couldn't even think where to put my basket of clean washing down! I also remembered telling my sister Sandy a few years before about a book I had read, named "How To Say No Without Feeling Guilty".

It took me a while to learn to do that myself, and here I was, allowing people to creep in, and try to lay a sense of guilt onto me if I didn't give in to their demands to be secretary for this or that, or treasurer for some other association. While it was flattering to a degree, I really learned the hard way years later, that it's not so much how trustworthy a person is (although being an honest person is a big plus, of course!), it's just that no one else wants to do the thankless task!

I remembered an extra job I was asked to do at around that time. A friend from our Poetry Society who was working in the Information Centre rang me to say they wanted to see me urgently and could I come into town? My mind had whisked through the things I could get done while I was in town, to save a bit of time, and so I agreed. What was the urgent thing they wanted to see me about? I asked.

"We'll talk to you about it when you come in," I was told.

Puzzled, I went to the Information Centre and was told that the Historical Society would like me to write a small book, larger than a booklet but not big enough to warrant the title of 'book' on the history of gold mining in the Buller District, to have it printed in time for their anniversary celebrations in two months' time. As the Buller District is steeped in fascinating gold mining history, it would have been a shame to do a quick job on the research, when, with more time for research, a decent-sized book could have been produced, and New Zealand-wide sales of this would have offset at least some of the cost of research, writing and printing.

"How much are you willing to pay to have this done?" I asked, already having a feeling of foreboding.

The man, whom I will call Rex, looked blank, and then embarrassed. It hadn't occurred to them that I should be paid, and for what would have been a lengthy and very time-consuming job which was expected to be completed in just two months!

"Er..." Rex began.

"Have you heard that phrase: 'a labourer is worthy of his hire'?" I asked. "In this case, *her* hire." Rex's face reddened. "I am a professional person Rex, and an extremely busy one and can't afford to do time-consuming jobs for nothing. This is how I make my living, by writing articles and books. I'm already working on the North School history, for which I am being paid."

"Yes, well..." he said, his face still flushed, and the other two people in the Information centre also looked embarrassed. I was shocked that they, of all people, had thought they could get a small book produced within a short time frame, and for nix.

"When you decide how much you can afford from the Information Centre funding to pay to have a small book produced, please get back to me," I said. I was disappointed in my friend, as he knew how hard I worked.

I was not at all surprised when they didn't get back in touch with me. I had heard that the Centre eventually had a tiny booklet printed, but I didn't want to know any more about it.

**

The days flew by, each merging into the next, but not with monotonous precision as the first part of this sentence may have suggested. But there seemingly was no division between night and day - one week to the next. I put this down to the amount of proofreading I had to do on the extensive North School history, and the work on other committees and associations I was involved with. Somewhere in the middle of all that I wrote articles for the Southerner newspaper; other South Island-wide and national newspapers and magazines, compiled the District Council newspaper, and contemplated my battle-scarred arms and hands.

I got better though, at learning to say no, albeit with still a small sense of guilt!

As time went by, Reilly changed very little in his habits. However, growth-wise, he had rocketed away. My kitten was barely a kitten anymore, barring his still kittenish habits. As previously mentioned, I had firmly decided from day one that Reilly was most definitely a 'he'. No female cat could possibly be as bad, I reasoned, except for Honeybelle of Mandalay. But for every rule, there must be an exception, mustn't there?

After his initial deep suspicion of the monster (me) in the bath, Reilly developed a fascination for water. That fascination is unchanged. As soon as he was old enough to leap onto the corner of the bath, he made a habit of it as soon as he heard the water running.

A softy at heart, I'd put a dry flannel on the corner for him to sit on. I could tell he appreciated that small favour. Enamel baths are notoriously cold in the winter. All the same, I was convinced he didn't approve of the colour of 'his' flannel. It was pink - one of my favourite colours.

"Why couldn't I have a blue one, or even a green one? Pink is sissy."

"I don't have either a blue flannel or a green one, and anyway, pink is the colour of love."

"Huh."

"You should be grateful, my arrogant young friend."

"I am, can't you tell? I still say I don't like this colour."

"You're supposed to be colour-blind."

"Don't believe all you read and hear, woman! I am a Super Cat!"

With that, he gave me an extra-aloof look and gazed at the ceiling, apparently intent on the slight mildew. I wasn't fooled. I climbed into the bath, my bath hat perched 'upstairs, downstairs' style on my head.

Reilly's expression was cynical. I do not claim by any means to be a perfect model for a soap ad, but I do wish he hadn't looked at me quite like that. As I am of a medium build, I could hardly say I felt *deflated*, but nevertheless, Reilly did cause me to feel inadequate.

I lay down in the bath; my scratches, courtesy of Reilly stung. He peered down at me, his eyes and ears alert at the patterns the suds made in the water, and the fascinating sounds the water made when I swished it around. He put a tentative paw on my shoulder. I knew he was longing to climb in, but water was still a bit of a mystery to him. He withdrew, sat on his pink flannel and contemplated my wriggling toes. They bore investigating, which he promptly did by walking down the side of the bath and daintily stepping over the taps to get as near as possible to those little toes. I popped them under the water and Reilly lost interest. He walked gingerly back up the side of the bath and neatly sat on his flannel. For a moment I watched him out the corner of my eye. Another minute passed by, then the tentative paw came out again to rest lightly on my shoulder.

"Come on in Reilly, the water's fine," I said quietly, trying not to giggle. I wriggled my fingers by my sides and Reilly stepped down to investigate. I dared not laugh as he walked across my stomach, ticklish though I am. I had no intention of giving him the chance to sink his claws in.

I gritted my teeth as Reilly's paws made interesting little craters in my stomach, which was just above water level. He watched the water lapping at my sides, his profile showing his lightly amused pussycat smile. He turned and plodded back up my stomach, sat on my chest, tucked his paws under, began purring, and settled down for a nap. His fur, only a breath away, tickled my nose. I didn't dare sneeze for fear of those claws sinking in.

Meanwhile, the water grew cold and I felt ripples of chill creeping over my flesh. Reilly purred and napped on.

"Who cares if I get chilled? Answer me that, cat!" I said into his fur.

Reilly opened one eye and turned it on me.

"You invited me to sit here."

"Well not *exactly*," I said aloud, absorbing his thoughts.

"It's called splitting straws."

"No it's not!" I said into his fur. He yawned, bored with me. "It's called - expecting me to lay here in this cold water while you decide to have a nap."

"You invited me in. 'Come on in' you said; 'the water's fine'," he reminded me.

I know I did but I didn't want him reminding me.

I slowly raised my hands, got Reilly in a firm grip and lifted him out of the bath.

"You could have given me at least ten minutes longer!"

"No I couldn't. That water's cold and I'm *freezing*!" Maybe the latter was a bit of an exaggeration but I figured it didn't hurt to exaggerate sometimes. Anyway, my teeth were chattering, so that justified my exaggeration. Reilly sat on the bath mat and washed at the wet places on his fur where I'd held him – and was completely disinterested in my condition.

On one occasion when Lou was visiting we were intrigued to see how far Reilly would go during an inspection of my bath water. We stood there quietly while Reilly sniffed at an awkward angle from the side of the bath.

"The water's fine, Reilly," I said softly, remembering what I'd said to him on his first excursion into the bath.

"Smells good too, although a bit sissy with that fancy stuff you put in."

He stretched a little further... then *splash*! In he went, and Lou and I smothered our laughter. Reilly calmly swam to the side and scrambled out, shaking his paws as he went.

He looked at us in a snooty manner.

"If you think that was accidental, you're wrong, wrong! I rather enjoyed that quick dip."

I looked at him disbelievingly and as if to stress his point, he shook one of his forepaws then proceeded to lick excess water from it.

**

Actually, I was delighted with Reilly's antics; after all, how many people can honestly say their cat joins them in the bath?

At one of my workplaces a few days later I rapturously told one of the two young men I shared an office with of my cat's unusual behaviour.

"He draped himself across my chest while I was in the bath and went to sleep!" I foolishly said.

The young man grinned wickedly.

"*I* wouldn't mind draping myself across your chest while you're in the bath, either!"

I blushed furiously and said: "I guess I asked for that, didn't I?"

He chuckled and walked away. Knowing the two men, I should have known better than to blurt out something like that, but once said, I couldn't undo it. Still, it *was* cute - the way Reilly joined me in the bath. I had never known such a cat before!

**

My friend Keith visited after work one day, to meet Lou, who only had a couple of days left before her departure back to Nelson was due. Keith took his big work boots off at the door and strode inside in his grubby overalls and filthy socks. He glanced at the empty bottle of Moet et Chandon Lou had brought with her as a gift for staying with me, and Keith commented that it was empty.

"It was full when I brought it down," Lou called out from the lounge.

"You girls been on the booze?" Keith wanted to know.

"One bottle of champers over several days?" I asked. "I think we've been very good, actually."

With a grunt of assent Keith put the bottle back on top of the fridge and took a couple of steps to the side to look at Lou, who was comfortably sitting in a plush armchair on the other side of the room. "So you're Lou," Keith said. "I've heard a lot about you."

"All good, I hope!" Lou jested.

"Sure, all good. That's why I've come to meet you!"

Just as he moved again he accidentally kicked over Reilly's saucer of milk. It spilled out onto the dreary Feltex carpet. I quickly fetched a cloth and mopped up the worst of the milk, my eyes crossing and nose twitching, as Keith was sorely in need of a bath, with special attention to his feet needed. I looked at Lou who was struggling not to laugh at me. Keith chattered on, oblivious.

Reilly came out from under the table to investigate. "Huh! Some friend! He just kicked over my saucer of milk. I saw him do it!"

"Yes I know, Reilly," I said, still scrubbing and mopping at the milk spill.

"What?" Keith said.

"She's talking to Reilly," Lou said, smiling.

I couldn't see from my position, on hands and knees on the floor, but I just knew that Keith had rolled his eyes.

"Did he answer?" he asked. I could hear the laughter in his voice.

"Not yet, but he will in a minute," I said lightly.

"He should be cleaning up the spilt milk himself!" Reilly said huffily.

"Reilly says you should have cleaned up the spilt milk yourself!" I said, grinning widely. My timing was out a little. It took barely ten seconds for Reilly to make a comment!

Keith glanced down at me. "Oh, I wondered what you were doing down there at my feet," he said saucily.

"Cleaning up spilt milk from Reilly's saucer and trying not to pass out," I riposted.

"Cheeky wench," Keith replied with a grin.

**

CHAPTER FIVE

Beach Adventure

I was running low on wood and coal and the nights were still cold enough to warrant getting further supplies in. I decided to pack up some plastic grocery bags and take a short car ride to the beach to fill them.

Reilly was outside, fidgeting; he knew I was going out. I watched him - my head at an angle while contemplating Reilly's next move.

"Do you want to go to the beach, Reilly?"

"Meow. I thought you'd never ask!"

I opened the door to my sports car.

"In you get."

He needed no second bidding. He leaped in and made himself comfortable in the back hatch, where he had a good view of what was going on outside.

"We're just going for a little ride," I soothed.

"I know that, woman. That's why I jumped into this car. So we could go to the beach. Lead on, McDuff! Is that how the saying goes? Never mind, drive on, woman."

I looked in the rear vision mirror and was amused at his aloof air. It was almost as if he was saying: "I do this all the time but it *does* tend to be a bore sometimes."

Despite the aloof look, I worried that Reilly might not enjoy the actual car ride to the beach, short though it was. It was barely five minutes' ride and I shouldn't have worried. Reilly was too interested in the new sights around us to be disturbed by the fact he was riding in a car, without the comforting restraints of being in a floor-padded cage, or even having a sheepswool rug to sit on.

When I opened the door, Reilly chirruped and galloped down the sandy laneway, his tail to one side in a frolicking gesture. He adored the beach. He spun around and around in the sand, leaped on driftwood and sharpened his claws in a frenzy of excitement, and then he dived back into the soft sand and rose up to delicately sniff the delicious, salt-laden air. I wondered how Reilly would cope with the sea. I left a couple of bags of driftwood at a strategic point on the beach and took a casual walk down to the ebbing tide. Looking back, I was pleased to see Reilly already well on his way to catching up with me. He appeared unconcerned about padding over wet sand. A few cursory sniffs at it: nothing rose up to bite or scare him; he continued on his way.

By now I was standing, gumboot-shod, in the shallow water. Reilly sensibly reasoned that if Mum could happily stand there in the water, then so could he.

The water was cold but he swam a short distance then returned, giving himself a quick shake before sitting on the wet sand to give himself an even quicker wash. He stood up, wet sand clinging to his fur. Again came that nonchalant look and it was obvious that I was more concerned about his bedraggled look than what *he* was.

Up the beach we plodded. A family group came down the track leading to the beach and, giggling, pointed at Reilly and me. I smiled.

"Is that a real cat?" The man asked, grinning.

"It sure is," I said.

"What's a cat doing swimming at the beach?" I was asked. Foolish question!

I replied simply: "because he enjoys it."

"Does he know he's a cat?"

"Of course, but he's no ordinary cat, y' know."

"We can see that!" Laughing, they moved off and looked back from time to time as if still disbelieving. I could hear their laughter carried on the breeze, even when they were well away from us. Reilly disdainfully watched them go until they were out of sight, and then he frolicked some more in the shallows while I finished collecting wood. Soon I had all I needed. I unlocked the car door and said: "hop in, Reilly. We're going home."

He promptly hopped in and sat in the passenger seat as most of the hatch area and back seat were taken up with bags of driftwood. Back home, Reilly flopped in front of the fire and snoozed. His first venture to the beach was not only very successful, he'd also shown a family he was "no ordinary cat" and put extra life and enjoyment into their day.

In the evening I played some of my CDs. When the song by Tina Turner "Simply The Best" was playing, Reilly sat up and stared intently at the stereo.

"They're playing my song, Ma! I hope you realize that it was written especially for *me.*"

"Of course I realized," I said, lightly sarcastic, and went back to my writing. Reilly gave me an arch look. I observed him, and considered his rapid growth and the fact that he was now old enough to seek out members of the opposite sex. He was also a fine looking young cat and what a shame it would be to have those wonderful looks marred by torn ears, scars, scratches, an over-sized head and a world-weary, belligerent look.

"Hmmm, young man, I think it's time we took you in for a little operation."

His eyes narrowed suspiciously. At eight months old he was magnificent, with a fine ruff already in evidence around his neck. His deep grey, silver and white coat - thick and lustrous - was a pleasure to touch, if he'd let you. But I could easily visualize him looking scruffy with torn ears and matted fur through weeks away 'tomcatting' if I didn't do something about it.

It was early November when I made an appointment with the vet and a few days later I told Reilly we were going for a nice little ride to town and that he was going to meet the nice vet.

"Nice, *nice?* We shall see. I'm very suspicious of you."

I tickled his nose through the cage and spoke reassuringly to him.

The vet admired him, saying: "he's been in a good paddock."

I felt like saying something smart, but curbed my tongue.

"When was he born?"

"March 17th, St Patrick's Day. That's as near as I can work it out."

"I think you could be right," I was told. "Is that why he's got an Irish name?"

"Yes," I said. "He's actually Seamus O'Reilly, but for convenience it's shortened to Reilly."

The vet looked at me disbelievingly. I could imagine what she might be thinking: *another one of these single potty women, dotty over a cat.*

Still, the vet was very pleasant, and smiled as he checked Reilly out.

**

Later on in the day, following a phone call from the vet nurse to tell me Reilly was awake, I returned to town and collected my cat. He glared at me.

"I will never trust another woman as long as I live. I intend to be as devious, cat-tankerous and demanding as it is possible to be. That will be my revenge, woman."

"You've had your revenge on me ever since you came to live here, cat. Look at the scars on my arms and hands! They might never go away!"

"I just wanna make sure you never forget me."

"There's no chance of that!"

The short exchange helped restore his dignity, but I continued to work on him by soothing him with soft words as I took the cage out on the back lawn. I opened the cage, prepared to gently lift

Reilly out but he leaped out and promptly sat down to wash his tender rear.

"Mummy's sorry puss, but I had to do it, for your own sake."

"Oh yeah?"

"Yes." I reached out to give him a gentle pat and was the immediate recipient of a quick swipe which left neat red-oozing lines down my hand.

"Charming!" I said sternly. "You're as tough as old boots!"

"Yeah, and don't you forget it. And don't forget I really know how to bear a grudge."

After a few days of glares however, he acted as if the whole incident was forgotten. Odd, sidelong glances kept me wary, though.

**

One crisp winter Saturday a few months earlier, I thought I'd take a break from writing to potter around in the garden. The weather, for a change, was clear. Weeding around the pelargoniums gave me a sense of pleasure and fulfillment. Pelargoniums have a fragrance that reminds me of bush walks on days long ago; giving me a beautiful nostalgic feeling.

I pulled out long grass and creeping plants from the garden. I looked in amusement at the sparse ground cover around the septic tank area. The humorous American writer Erma Bombeck who, some years back wrote a book about the grass being greener around the septic tank should have taken a look at this, I thought.

Out came a few more weeds from the garden.

"Hi! You look busy!"

It was the Avon lady, out for a walk with her husband and baby, and their Golden Labrador dog Boof. I went over to chat to them. The young woman's eyes swiveled to the furry bundle of Reilly who had poked his nose between the slats of the fence, then hopped up onto the first piece of cross framing timber. The young Labrador ambled over to assess the goings-on; Reilly leaped down to the outside path and, hissing, stalked towards him. Boof's happy face disappeared in a look of puzzlement.

"I only wanted to say hello."

"Hello. Now buzz off buster. Youse on my territory."

"That's not nice. I don't think I want to know you."

"Good. The best end of a dog is his rear, when it's retreating at top speed, that is. I wanna see your rear."

"You're disgusting! My mother always told me to be careful of rough cats like you!"

"Your mother is a smart dame, even if she *is* a dog. Vamoose, pooch!"

"I hope we never meet again, woof, woof!"

He backed away and ran off. Reilly eyed his retreating rear.

"Hiss, snarl. You're so good looking!"

I felt ashamed. I had been about to say hello to Boof.

"Reilly, how could you speak so rudely to a nice young dog like that?"

"Didn't you ask de Good Lord for a tough tomcat?"

"Well..." I began, aware of the odd looks I was receiving.

"Well, a tough tomcat is what you wanted and a tough tomkitten you got. All I gotta do is some more growin'. Ain't I provin' meself?"

I apologized to the young family.

"Please excuse my little cat. He doesn't seem to know he's only four months old."

The young woman smiled sweetly. She, Debbie, is also a cat lover.

"It's good to see he can stick up for himself though, isn't it?"

"Yes," I agreed. "But not *that* well!"

Their dog Boof moved forward to investigate any proceedings. "Woof."

"Hiss, snarl. I don't care if you *are* the dog of my mother's friends. You gotta understand, dis is *my* territory."

Boof, however, was not convinced. He moved closer and withdrew quickly as a sharp claw whizzed past his black muzzle. He retreated behind his master, Pete, and glared at Reilly from a safe distance. Reilly out-glared him.

"Well, we'd better be off," Debbie said, beginning to push their infant son along in his pushchair.

"Oh please!" I begged. "Don't let my awful little cat chase you away!"

"Oh no," Debbie said, her smile waning. "We had to go anyway."

When Pete had walked with Boof a few meters back down the footpath, they turned to wait for Debbie to catch up. Boof, still skulking behind his master, stepped out to one side and barked several times. It was a safe enough distance from which to voice his disapproval of Reilly's unwelcoming attitude.

I told Reilly off as I returned to pick up the weeds. I felt almost as if *I* had given my friends a poor reception.

"Dat's gratitude for you, woman! Either I'm here to do your dirty work for you, or I move out!"

"You wouldn't do that! No one would *have* you!" I stood up, my hands on my hips, and watched him playing in the pile of weeds.

"Oh yeah?"

"Yeah. You know when you're well off."

"Course I do. I'm not stupid."

"I never said you were. Now come on, Reilly. Get out of that pile. I want to dump it."

"This is good to play in."

"Maybe so, but I'm not leaving it there for your convenience."

"Killjoy."

"Where did you learn such awful language at such a tender age?"

"I was brought up tough and then abandoned. Dat meant I had to learn to be even tougher. It's a hard world out there, woman."

"Don't I know it!" I stood there for a few more minutes while Reilly rummaged through the pile of weeds and then, tiring of his game, he leaped away to investigate a small spider crawling up the side of the house. I bundled up the weeds and moved towards the compost heap, Reilly turning and leaping at the long stalk of grass trailing from the bundle.

He caught my leg with his claws.

"Ow! Get off!" My leg began to sting almost immediately. *Oh Lord*, I quietly prayed. *I had been told to be careful of what I prayed for; that I might get more than what I bargained for. You were right. I've prayed for patience and oh how I've had patience! Only two months or so down the track; my arms and legs are a mess and my friends are giving up coming to see me. Do you know what they say, Lord? Well you would, wouldn't you? Because you're all-seeing, all-powerful. They say things like: I'll only come to see you if your cat's tied up, or if he's left home, or you've hired him out as a killer for a few weeks.*

It's humiliating, that's what it is.

Do you have dog doings on your lawn? came a voice from somewhere. I had to concede the voice was God's.

"No," I replied and dumped the weeds in the sagging compost bin.

You prayed for a huge tomcat to keep dogs away, did you not?

"Yes I did," I admitted, not caring to be reminded yet again. Reilly had reminded me only a short while before.

I have repaid you tenfold, said the Lord.

I nodded despairingly. "Indeed You have."

Be careful of what you pray for. God really *does* have a sense of humour!

And indeed, Reilly *is* ten cats rolled into one, with the superior qualities of cartoon cats Horse and Garfield overruling. What a deadly combination - the superior strength, cunning and meanness of Horse combined with the biting sarcasm, cunning, gluttony and meanness of Garfield, and with the subtle additions of an enquiring, loving nature - subtle enough to suck me in every time!

I reminded myself however, that Reilly does not like lasagne, and I have never seen him catch an eel. Mice, birds, lizards, beetles, moths and the like, but not eels. All the same, I cannot rule out eels. It would not surprise me one day if he *did* bring home a big eel.

Be careful of what you pray for.

That phrase came to me again a day or so later when Reilly brought home an eel, of about one meter in length. I wondered if he had caught it himself.

"Did you catch this yourself, Reilly?" I asked. Reilly and his eel were on the back lawn.

Reilly munched sickeningly into the eel and stopped for a moment to look at me, pieces of eel incongruously hanging from both sides of his mouth.

"Maybe I did, and maybe I didn't," he replied, and licked around his mouth. The bits of eel disappeared and he bent over to have another bite of the eel.

"A simple yes or know would have sufficed," I said.

"Probably," he said between mouthfuls, but didn't enlarge further.

I suspected that he might have discovered it and worked on the premise of 'when opportunity knocks, make sure you open the door.' I could easily visualize a cat such as one in similar appearance to the very tough cartoon character of Horse, catching one eel and then going back for another and while he, Horse was about to catch the next one, Reilly 'happened along' and took the opportunity of stealing it.

"I think you could be an opportunist, cat," I said, smiling.

But Reilly would not be drawn on that. He simply replied: "I am a Super Cat, woman, and don't you forget it!"

"As if I ever could!" I retorted and went inside to get the sound and image out of my head of Reilly crunching his way through the eel.

**

Debbie's and Pete's animals had their revenge on Reilly soon afterwards when I paid them a visit. Reilly had decided to come too but was very quickly and unceremoniously ushered off, after first being treed by their big fluffy ginger cat then, when Reilly ran down the tree, chased by Boof. Debbie looked embarrassed and said she felt awful.

"Don't worry about it," I said. "After all, Reilly was so awful the other day when you came past my place. Your animals are just getting their own back, and they're working together on it. When I lived in Nelson I remember a neighbour whose dog and cat worked in tandem to get food. The cat would climb up into the pantry to the top shelf to knock down a thawing piece of lamb or beef, and the dog would help the cat demolish it, or at least as much of it that wasn't still frozen, and demolish it before the owner came back. The owner only realized that's how her meat was disappearing when she came home early and caught them at it."

Debbie chuckled at that. "It sounds like a wife coming home early and catching her hubby out."

"Kind of. Caught in the act, eh?'

Debbie chuckled again.

When I left, I looked around for Reilly. I couldn't see him anywhere and called him as I walked home. He emerged from the long grass at the back of the Post Office welfare cottage and gave a yawn.

"Got your come uppance, cat!" I said, pleased and relieved to see him all the same.

He, tender age that he was at, still managed to give me a haughty look that contained all the superciliousness developed in cats down through the ages.

"I look on it purely as a bit of exercise."

He ran off ahead, the incident apparently forgotten, and then stopped to turn and wait for me.

"What's for tea, woman?"

It came back to me: *be careful of what you pray for.*

**

CHAPTER SIX

Return To The Beach

When I had decided that Reilly had more than fully recovered from his little 'weight loss', I took him to the beach again. It was as if he actually *expected* a ride in the car. Or maybe it was the sight of my little red gumboots that did it. I only donned them if I was going to the beach or going onto a farm during the course of an interview in wet weather, or knew that I would be crossing muddy paddocks, or maybe all three.

I collected up plastic shopping bags, put them in the car and returned for my cat.

"Want to go to the beach, Reilly?"

He sat up from his comfortable place on the sofa and meowed.

"Of *course* I do. When opportunity knocks, one does not close the door, does one?"

"Only if you're foolish," I grinned, understanding completely, and thinking back to the eel episode. I don't think Reilly realized that he had, in a round about way, agreed with me then. In fact, he seldom liked to agree with me. It was as if he thought that by being in agreement with me, it was somehow showing a weakness.

Reilly leaped into the car as if he had been doing that same thing for years, and off we went. As we drove I was reminded of the time not long before when he went missing. I had looked everywhere - even down the toilet, which is one of his favourite 'watering holes'.

"Tastes far better than out of a plastic bowl, woman!" he would say.

The cat was nowhere to be seen. I had asked several neighbours if they'd seen him - no, they hadn't. I went for a walk down the street and around the block - still no Reilly. I returned, scratches and bites forgotten and my heart heavy, and took another circuit of the house. I glanced into the car and there he was, sitting up and yawning.

Oh, I remember it well.

"Yawn. You weren't looking for me by any chance, were you, woman?"

Relieved, I opened the door. I don't know why I hadn't checked my car out properly earlier. He'd hopped through a window, open obviously just far enough for him to squeeze through. I would never have guessed that he could get through such a small gap, but squeeze through is what he did. I made a fuss of him, thrilled to know that he was okay.

"Errgh! Gerroff!"

And then the inevitable happened. He bit me.

**

We arrived at the beach. It was a grey day but quite mild and I was filled with a mixture of pleasure and resignation at the chore ahead. Pleasure - at the joy Reilly would have in frolicking around, and resignation - at the wood I'd have to search for. Most of the driftwood was too small and rotten, or else far too large.

I filled the shopping bags, taking them back to the car two at a time. Meanwhile, Reilly kept up his frolicking. The morning cooled and the wind swept down the beach. Reilly's long fur fanned out, showing the white underneath. He looked glorious as he held up his head and sniffed at the wind, deciphering the many scents it carried. I filled up a few more bags, hoping to get the job finished before it began to rain. Reilly leaped up and away into the pampas and on my last load I called him. He wasn't around anywhere. With aching arms I trudged back to the car, and there he was, sitting on top of it.

What a delight he looked, his magnificent colouring a perfect foil against the ruby red of my car. I wrote this poem in memory of that day, and of the occasions following when Reilly did the same thing.

Cat On A Warm Car Roof

Such pleasure the cat discovers -
leaping and turning with all
the dexterity of an acrobat:
all this combined with untapped
artistic talent
in the whirls and swirls
he makes in the gold-flecked ironsand.

What unparalleled joy
to leap onto jutting driftwood
silhouetted in its death mask
against the watery sun,
and sink into
ess-blasted (sun, sea, sand and salt) wood.
Reilly's glorious greys,
all at once a foil and yet a blend
of those colours
that mark an overcast day
at Carter's Beach.

Then, when her wood-gathering
is near done,
she pauses to admire the cat;
who frisks again and leaps away
into katipo country -
windswept pampas at beach edge.

She admires the scene once more,
calls her cat who is

nowhere to be seen,
and returns to the car,
arms aching with wood-weight.
There Reilly sits on the warm car roof;
he meows in greeting:
look, I'm better than any dog!
The cat on a warm car roof,
glorious greys against ruby red;
so pleasing to the eye,
and indeed he lifts the day
away from despondent hues.

**

One crisp morning I was back collecting driftwood at the beach. Reilly cavorted happily in the pampas and with chirrups, leaped up and down ancient drift logs. Collecting wood was harder this time, as the sand was so soft and trudging through it with laden bags was very tiring. As I bent over to top up a bag I thought: *I hope no one is silly enough to come driving down here.*

Barely had the thought been established in my mind when I heard the faint drone of a vehicle being driven slowly down the laneway. I willed the driver not to come any further but alas, the vehicle continued on its way, came into view and then stopped - the motor revving. It was a rental station wagon with three Indian people on board. Well and truly stuck in the soft sand, not even practical methods of putting sacks and small sticks under the wheels helped to get the vehicle unstuck.

I offered to get other help and the driver, a young lawyer with a strong American accent was most grateful. I told Reilly to stay and keep the people company and so he did. They were all most intrigued with him. The other two people were the young man's parents who had moved to the States many years before and had raised their son there. Although the parents still spoke minimal English, their faces at Reilly's antics told their own story.

"I'll show these new humans just what a cat can do!"

And indeed he did. He chirruped, frolicked and leaped over logs and tufts of grass, and when I looked back he seemed perfectly content to entertain.

Several trips later to the nearby dairy for telephoned assistance, the station wagon was finally pulled out of the soft sand, but not before a four wheel drive vehicle had also become stuck in an attempt to tow the station wagon out. A local man was contacted and barreled his tractor down the beach. It was obvious he'd had to tow vehicles out of the sand several times before and he did not look too pleased at having to do it again. I didn't blame him, as there were notices up in clear view, warning of the danger of driving into soft sand. It was as if those who glanced at them thought: "pah! It can't happen *to us!*"

I had to leave as I had other work to do, but before I left, I asked the young man if he would mind giving me a call to let me know if they were okay. He did so, and was most grateful for the help given. Not only that, they were amazed at my cat and the things he did. They had never seen anything like it before.

"Reilly is no ordinary cat," I said yet again.

"Yeah, we sure could see that!" he said in his strong accent. "It's like he's from another planet!"

Maybe he was right.

It had been a most unusual morning, one I remember well, years later.

**

Reilly's leaping and cavorting had results in many varied directions. Apart from leaping onto the bench or the stove, he developed the habit of leaping onto the drapes; his initial leap had to be at the highest point possible. Fortunately, the habit was reasonably short-lived. He grew so big and solid that future repeats of the same would have resulted in wrenching the rails from their brackets and bringing all to the floor.

At first I'd thought his drape-leaping habit was because he'd seen a fly, but I soon realized that it was simply for the sheer hell of it.

REILLY : TARZAN OF THE DRAPES !

"A PIN !!...DROPPED!..DOWN THERE....."

The thermal drapes, although second hand, were still in good condition when I was given them. Reilly left his legacy - tiny holes, that let in pin point stars of light. "Reilly wuz here" those pin-prick holes could have declared, in a form of inverted Braille. To accompany his 'declaration' was the inevitable small swatch of fur from his neck ruff.

That neck ruff: he hated it the first year it grew.

He looked magnificent, but his obvious awareness of his magnificence did not override the annoying factors of his ruff. Factor One: in washing himself, his tongue did not reach beyond the end of his long ruff. He constantly tried to spit out clinging wet fur. Factor Two: despite the added warmth and esteem the ruff gave him, there were times when the ruff was *too* hot. Solution? Thin it out by way of sharp tugs with his wonderful fangs. Result? Tufts and swatches of white and soft grey fur lying around the house; clinging to the sides of chairs, on the mats, carpet, bed - and anywhere else he decided was a suitable place to rid himself of his extra long fur.

"Well, what else could you expect? If it's good enough for you human types to tear your hair out it's good enough for we superior beings to rid ourselves of excess fur. Simple, isn't it?"

"I already knew that," I said dryly.

"So why the monologue?"

"To explain to others who do not have the superior wit or charm to realize it for themselves." I kept my face bland.

He eyed me suspiciously.

"Humans or cats?"

"Whichever," I said.

Reilly glared, sure that there was sarcasm in my voice. Was there? If there was, perhaps I was picking up *his* bad habits.

**

Out of the frying pan....

Reilly could not resist leaping onto the stove, despite repeated warnings of "HOT! STAY OFF!"

"You can't fool *me.* A few sniffs and I can soon tell whether or not an element is switched on. Give me credit for intelligence, woman!"

His leaping was generally done from the back of a dining chair. He would balance precariously, leaning forward with a twitching nose to test the warmth of the air above the stove. All elements switched off, he would leap onto the stove and perch neatly over an element and stare out the window.

"Get *off,* Reilly!"

"Why should I? We cats like to observe general goings-on from a high vantage point."

"*I* know that!"

"Then leave me alone. Can't you see I'm concentrating?"

Exasperated, I would lift him off and incur his wrath.

He gave up leaping onto the stove, at least for a while, the day he landed in a frying pan. His head lowered and his bottom wriggling, he made the leap. I had my mouth open ready to warn him but too late! With a splash he landed in the frying pan on the stove. The pan had been left soaking with water in it to soak off scrambled egg residue.

He looked so ridiculous that I had to laugh.

"Serves you right," I said. "Lucky for you the stove wasn't switched on."

Reilly gave me a lofty look.

"If it was, I would have known it and would not have made that leap. How dare you leave a dirty frying pan on the stove?"

And with each paw raised and shaken in turn, he elegantly stepped out and walked down the bench, leaving a trail of scrambled egg and sand-dotted prints for me to clean up. With a chirrup and a final leer, he sped around the corner into the lounge and leaped onto the free-standing, empty fireplace, to sink down in an attitude of great repose.

"You see? It's all elementary, woman, and what a great pun I made! Element-ary, get it?"

I stood there in front of the fireplace and laughed. "Of course," I said. "What a punster you can be!"

And what a cat, I thought.

I wrote another poem, reminiscent of *Cat On A Warm Car Roof.*

Cat On A Cold Metal Stove

He sits on the stove
a picture of beauty
and yet amusement, and stares
around in aloofness and cat humour
at his creative effect.
....He's well aware the fire is not yet lit.
He sniffs the air around the oven;
it too, is cold.
He leaps to a good vantage point
from where he can watch the passersby.
He lands with agile grace
into the frying pan, there to soak.
He stands and summons a look
as much to say:
"So what! I do this every day!"
With an elegant shaking of each paw
he grandly steps out;
the stage is clear -
the audience agog;
he runs along the bench
and leaps away, back to the fireplace
to start again.
He gives a smug meow which says it all:
he makes a mockery
of: out of the frying pan into the fire!

**

Sitting and playing in boxes and cartons is one of a cat's favourite pastimes, and Reilly was no exception. Of course it *would* have to be a box of important papers or a box of computer paper. The very least I could have hoped for was that Reilly had clean paws while he set himself up for a cozy nap. But did he have clean paws? Not on your nellie! I had long ago decided that this was one of Reilly's strategies on "how to get even with humans".

And paper was *wonderful* stuff, especially if it was slightly rumpled (by You-Know-Who), for tearing to pieces and spitting out. Sometimes my only warning that Reilly had pushed open the office door and entered the out of-bounds room, was the sudden rustling of paper, followed quickly by tearing and spitting sounds. That meant I had to run, lest Reilly had sunk his fangs into important documented material I needed in support of my writing work.

Reilly always had a smug look about him when I caught him with wet chunks of paper strewn around him, further convincing me of his desire to "get even" with we humans.

**

One Sunday afternoon big Mike visited again. I hadn't seen him for months and was pleased when he arrived. As I was coming to expect, Mike promptly asked after Reilly.

"How's that cat of yours? Where is he?"

Reilly, looking gorgeous, appeared at the ranchslider door and stared at us.

"Wow, he's grown! What a beautiful cat." He opened the door and bent down to the beguiling Reilly. "Oh, aren't you gorgeous?" he crooned. Reilly rubbed up against him and Mike put out his hand to stroke the soft fur.

"Be careful," I warned.

Too late. Reilly sank his claws into Mike's hand.

"Still a little bastard, I see," Mike said, but not without amusement in his voice. And the admiration was still there.

A few months later Mike visited me again. Well, I *thought* it was me he had come to visit, but I should have realized whom. Almost immediately after he'd said hello and taken off his safety helmet he asked, "Where's the famous Reilly?"

The cat appeared as if by magic and took Mike's admiration as his due.

"Is he still as handy with his teeth and claws?"

"Yes," I replied. "He sure is. Only now he's *worse.*"

"How do you mean? How could he possible be worse?"

"He's that much bigger!"

Mike laughed. "Give him a few more months of growing, put a chain around his neck and you could take him pig hunting!"

It was easy to visualize and we both laughed. Reilly looked at us as if we were far, far beneath him.

"I don't appreciate being laughed at."

"No cat does," I said quickly, and Mike gave me an odd look.

Reilly nonchalantly licked a paw.

"I'm not just an *ordinary* cat, y' know."

I grinned. "Haven't you just said a mouthful?"

"What?" Mike said, puzzled.

"I'm just talking to my cat," I said.

"That figures."

**

REILLY — SUFIE-CAT.

"DINCHA SEE A CAT SWIM BEFORE?"

CHAPTER SEVEN

Music to Soothe the Soul (And Cat)

When Reilly was just a few months old he showed a strong interest in music - not just *any* sort of music; it had to be easy listening. As I had mentioned earlier, Tina Turner made him sit up and take notice, so I figured that although he liked easy listening music, his taste ran to soul and blues. Or any other music that in usual terms defied categorization - as long as it didn't evoke restlessness or depression - or sheer rage, Reilly was all for it.

So I would slot a CD in the stereo and set it running, then pick up Reilly. He knew what was coming.

"In a soppy mood again, woman?"

"Yes, you could say that," I would say softly. Reilly would sink into my shoulder and begin to rumble with pleasure as we moved slowly around the room in a slow, relaxed twirl. Reilly's rumbling would grow louder, the vibrations felt strongly through my shoulder.

One evening after a few minutes he decided he'd had enough and would prefer to sit and watch me.

"Daft woman."

"So? You enjoyed dancing up until now."

He settled comfortably into the crocheted rug on the sofa.

"I still say you're daft."

"I don't care," I said dreamily, swaying in the glow of the firelight. I lost myself in the rhythm of the music and the ethereal quality of my own shadow flickering on the wall. I wrote a poem to reflect what I had felt at the time.

Dancing Shadows

In the firelight glow she began to dance
to the haunting music;
her movements an echo of it: the intangible
with the tangible, yet merging
into one entity.
She moved away from the firelight glow -
closer to the wall opposite;
her shadow was smaller and more defined.
Looking up, she realized that
her head was the focus in that
a round brass wall plaque
was centered over it:
a gladiator of sorts?
Some sort of omen? she thought.
What could I call myself?
A goddess of war,
dancing a war dance
to evoke the gods of battle?

And in the meantime the big cat
observed her, his great golden eyes
showing the wisdom of millenniums;
his humour overriding ancient cat memories:
light intrusive in already-golden orbs.

**

"I say it again woman, you're daft."

I stopped, the beautiful mood vanishing and with its departure, a sense of disappointment washed over me.

"And *I* say it again, cat. I don't care. You spoilt a good mood."

I swear it; Reilly grinned, a malicious light appeared in his eyes - or should I have blamed that light on the still-flickering fire? I started the CD playing again and sought to restore the mood. It was lost.

"Ah well, another evening, maybe."

"Yeah, not tonight, Josephine."

I spun around. "Where did you hear *that* phrase?"

The light caught Reilly's eyes again.

"You should know, woman. We cats have been around a very long time."

"As if I didn't know," I said shortly.

Reilly yawned, the action relaxed and luxurious. I stared, yet again admiring his wonderful *being*.

"I *know* that you know. I'm just reiterating it."

"Very clever with words, cat."

This time he looked insolent.

"Must I reiterate yet again?"

"No, you must not!" I said quickly, and found something else to do. The evening had gone flat, but the memory of it - at least the best part has remained very clear. *And probably for Reilly too, since he's so clever!* I thought grumpily.

**

Lou telephoned to say she was coming to Westport, and how was Reilly?

"His usual self. I'm bearing the scars still!" I laughed.

There was a slight pause.

"I suppose you've often thought of Reilly as a mixed blessing," she ventured.

I laughed again. "I sure have, but I'll say this for him, he sure has a strong personality!"

"That's what saved him," Lou replied. "He was determined to live, and to avenge himself on people for the way he was treated."

I agreed wholeheartedly. I just wished he wouldn't carry on his grudge for so long!

When Lou arrived, naturally Reilly was into mischief, so I put him outside. He stared back at me through the ranchslider, his eyes huge and forlorn.

"What a mean old mother you are, for putting the kitten outside. Just look at that sad little face!" Lou exclaimed.

Indeed Reilly *did* appear to have a sad little face.

"That's part of his act," I said, amused.

Lou slid the door open to let him back inside. He leaped in, a bundle of fluffy delight - until he sank his claws into Lou's ankle.

"See what I mean?" I said smugly.

Lou saw.

Later on during that visit, Lou was chatting to Reilly and, encouraged by the attention she gave him, he took a swipe at her. Lou leaped back, but not quickly enough. Who can estimate a cat's speed? 'Like lightning' is probably the closest term. Lou went home with a smarting scratch on the end of her nose, and I'd swear to the smirk I saw sneaking over Reilly's face. He sat back and began the process of washing himself. It was in his quick, lightly veiled glance that one could have interpreted him as saying: - 'that'll learn ya!'

I'd like to think that Reilly didn't have *everything* all his own way; Lou was able to take some delightful photographs of him. I felt however, that Reilly was secretly pleased at his brief stint as a model, so maybe Reilly did have everything his own way after all.

**

About two months later, Lou returned, this time with husband Dave. He was a member of a visiting pool team playing on the Coast. He and Lou were in fine form, both glad to get away from the confines and demands of running their very busy tavern in Nelson. That night they slept in my bed, while I slept with Reilly in the spare bedroom. In the morning he paid them a visit. I waited for it - both animal lovers, I knew Lou and Dave would be delighted with Reilly's growth rate. First came the endearment.

"What a gorgeous kitty cat you are, Reilly!" Dave exclaimed.

"He sure has grown," Lou commented. "He's *gorgeous!*"

Then: "ow, ow!" Dave complained loudly. "Well, I knew he was a little bastard, but you didn't tell me just *how* much of a bastard, Lou! Just *look* at my hands!"

Lou chuckled, her chuckles punctuated with a few "ows" of her own when Reilly leaped on her. Lying in the bed in the next room, I was highly amused. Hadn't I already gone through months of the same thing?

"I can't stand this!" Dave exclaimed. "I'm getting out of bed before Reilly tears me to bits!"

"Me too," Lou said.

When Dave emerged from the bedroom, I had already been up for a few minutes and was wondering what damage Reilly had done.

"Look at my hands!" Dave said, holding them out for inspection.

"It's dishwashing, Madge," I said with a grin, making reference to an old ad for dish washing detergent.

"Dishwashing? It's that *cat* of yours! He's a menace! I don't know how you put up with him. He was bad enough as a tiny kitten!"

"I had that figured out," I said.

Lou, who was still getting dressed, called out from the bedroom. "Don't tell her too much, Dave! She might want us to take Reilly back with us!"

**

There were many times when I truly believed I needed 'time out' from my (by now) big cat. If I traveled out of the district on business or family matters (generally both), Reilly went to 'Aunty Lois', who was always kind and accommodating. On my return after two or three days away she would say things like: "I had to let him out for a run", or "he's got a lot of energy, hasn't he?" or "what a strong personality!" and "I nearly fell over him several times. He's got this habit of running in front of you and banging into your legs, hasn't he?"

"Oh yes," I would say, and nod with grim humour. I've lost count of the times *I've* nearly fallen over him.

Meanwhile, it had been good to have that 'time out', even if just for a few days. All the same, I had to admit to missing Reilly intensely when I was away.

There were many occasions when I wasn't traveling out of the district and when Reilly was going through phases of being particularly bad, I could have done with 'time out' then. I asked my friend Keith if he would like to take Reilly for a bit of company, and to give Reilly a bit of a holiday.

Keith, who also had been the recipient of many scratches and 'hookings', wasn't fooled for a moment.

"No thanks! Some holiday it would be! What do you think I am? A masochist or something? Anyway, can you imagine how he and Ginger would get on?" Ginger was Keith's tough, but aging cat. He was already about 19, but that didn't stop him being tough!

I tried not to smile. "Reilly would want to be boss of the whole establishment."

My friend nodded sagely.

"That's what I mean! They would fight like cat and dog...er, cat and cat!"

Those people who mentioned vaguely they wouldn't mind having a cat were, to coin a phrase, *pounced* on.

"Would you like to borrow Reilly for a little while?" I would suggest in what I thought was my most persuasive manner.

For those who knew Reilly, their smiles would fade and they would emit body signals which were easily interpreted as: "keep that cat away from us!" And then they would leave soon afterwards, perhaps beating a hasty retreat in case I managed to persuade them into taking Reilly home with them for a few days.

I guess you could term their reaction as: "thrice bitten, thrice clawed, many times shy."

For those who didn't know what Reilly could be like, and had only seen him as a magnificent, fluffy cat, looked at me in amazement.

"What? A beautiful cat like that? How could you bear to be parted from him for even a day?"

Easy, I would think grimly.

"Oh no," they would shake their heads. "We couldn't take such a beautiful cat away from you, even for a day. You'd miss him far too much!"

Oh yeah? I'd think - scratches still stinging and fingertips throbbing where Reilly had hooked a claw down the sides of several fingernails.

As those various people would walk away on one occasion or another, it would occur to me that maybe Reilly's reputation had preceded him and those people weren't as innocent as they'd made out. Could that be true?

No, surely not!

In fairness to Reilly, there were a few people left who were prepared to put up with his behaviour, recognizing the wonderful cat within.

"Sensible people!" I imagine Reilly saying. "I really am the most *adorable* cat!"

One of those people was Jerome Moss, a young, immensely talented photographer who liked to visit for a chat, and have a play with Reilly. Jerome was fascinated by the feisty, fearless kitten, and spent around an hour one day, photographing Reilly in a series of play modes. Reilly was then aged around four months. I was enchanted with the scene; the large young man sprawled contentedly on my lounge floor, photographing the kitten from various angles. Reilly equally enjoyed the attention and posing for the camera.

The photograph Jerome presented to me a few days later was a delight. He had captured all the mischief of a kitten, and despite the encroaching sleepiness, the glint was still in Reilly's golden eyes.

Sadly, Jerome died some months later following a small plane crash, but I remember the day he happily lounged on my floor and captured Reilly on film as clearly as if it happened yesterday.

**

REILLY — HOOD ORNAMENT

"HANGING FOUR!"

CHAPTER EIGHT

Birthday Cat

Reilly's first birthday (in our years) drew near. I telephoned my friend Keith to ask if he'd like to come around to my place for a little party I intended putting on for Reilly.

"When is it?" I could hear the amusement in his voice.

"It's on the seventeenth," I said.

"What do you want to put on a party for a *cat,* for?"

"Because it's going to be his birthday," I said succinctly.

"You don't have birthdays for cats!"

"*You* mightn't, but *I* do! And so do other people. Anyway, it's a bit of fun and life's for living. Will you come around? Who knows, you might even enjoy yourself!"

Keith laughed, said he'd come around after work, and rang off. I visualized him shaking his head and chuckling merrily.

True to his word, Keith arrived, and looked at me as if I had a 'screw loose' when I produced Reilly's "cake", neatly presented on a flat round plastic tray.

I'd made the cake from raw minced meat and covered it with whipped cream. Sounds revolting? Not to a cat who has a penchant for raw minced meat and also for cream! In the centre of the cake I had placed a green candle. I lit it.

"Would you hold Reilly for me please?" As I carefully placed the cake in front of my cat, Keith looked at me as if I really had lost my marbles. I didn't care. It was worth it for the fun I was having. "Happy birthday to you, happy birthday to you, happy birrr-thday dear Reilly, happy birthday to you!" I sang cheerfully. Keith's face was a study of embarrassment and amusement.

Reilly stared suspiciously at the candle, his eyes big and round, his nose twitching.

"There's something pretty good here, but I don't think I like the look of that flickering orange thing on the end of that little green stalk. Hey! How did I know that? Aren't we cats supposed to be colour blind with some of the colours? Oh, yes that's right, *I'm* an exception to the rule because I'm a Super Cat!"

He sat back for a few seconds and looked smug.

Keith arched one eyebrow at me. I knew he was feeling foolish.

"You can blow the candle out for him Keith, if you like."

Keith gave me that certain look again, but did as I suggested, and then pulled the tiny green candle from the 'cake'.

Reilly wolfed down his cake.

"Not bad, not bad. I think I'd like another birthday next week."

"The novelty would wear off," I said.

"What?" Keith said, surprised at my apparent train of thought.

"I was talking to Reilly."

Keith gave me another 'you've got a screw loose' look. "That figures," he said. And he said those words just like big Mike had said.

I gave Reilly a catnip mouse which he promptly chewed, kicked at, rolled on and generally behaved in much the same way all cats do when given a new catnip mouse.

As Keith was about to leave, he suddenly stopped just inside the doorway and said: "Hey...I thought you said Reilly's birthday is on St Patrick's Day?"

"It is."

"Well, it's only the seventeenth of *February.*"

"I know," I grinned. "But if I'd waited until St Pat's Day, you wouldn't have come around to Reilly's party."

He laughed merrily. "And you say *I'm* cunning!"

"If you remember, I said it was going to be Reilly's birthday. I didn't remind you of what actual *month* we're in!

It had almost become a joke between us, that every St Patrick's Day we had - shall we say - a difference of opinion for one reason or another. We put it down to our dual Irish heritage.

When Keith left, grinning and still with a tinge of embarrassment colouring the tops of his cheeks, Reilly was still rolling and swiping at the mouse. It was strongly reminiscent of Christmas, when 'Aunty' Lou had sent him his very own gift. I'd held it up to him.

"Look Reilly, Aunty Lou has sent a gift *especially* for you!"

Reilly had taken a sniff, and then out came the claws and in a few short series of motions, the fancy wrapper was off and the contents - a catnip mouse and a small packet of special cat bites (delicious little biscuits for the discerning cat) were revealed.

**

Oh the capers Reilly got up to! A day never seemed to go by without him doing something either drastic or downright hilarious. Getting in not only my car, but other people's cars too, was a habit of his, and has caused much laughter and/or exasperation.

My friend Jan visited, occasionally with her beautiful, gentle collie named Jay. I generally had to warn Reilly to leave Jay alone. The beautiful dog would look woebegone, as much to say: "what did I do to deserve this?"

Not a thing, you lovely dog, I told her in my mind. *It's just that you're a dog.*

On one occasion when Jan came inside by herself to 'shout' me an early breakfast of croissants while I supplied the coffee, Jan left an hour later to visit another of her friends who lived a short distance away around the corner. Jay was sitting in the back, looking quite pleased to be leaving.

Reilly was perched on the bonnet of Jan's car.

"Get off, Reilly!" I said sternly.

He looked at me, insulted.

"I am warming my rear, I will have you know."

"I don't care if you are warming your rear, get off! Jan wants to leave!"

Jan got into her car. "He'll soon shift when I start it up."

"Don't be too sure," I said.

She carefully backed out my drive, Reilly enjoying his ride; sitting there like the majestic animal he is. When Jan put her car into first gear I thought Reilly would leap off but no, he rode all the way around to the next place, which was still in my line of vision. And he held that majestic position all the way there!

I was doubled over with laughter and my neighbour across the street told me later how she observed me laughing when Reilly went for a ride.

"What a weird cat you've got," she commented, looking at me sideways. Did she wonder if the 'weirdness' was catching? Never mind, it didn't bother me. I was too busy enjoying Reilly's latest little drama.

When Reilly came home a bit later on, he said it was rather nice 'leading the pack'!

I have Jan in mind when I write this: it was Arts Council night, and although I had not said anything, it was also the anniversary of my birthday as well as fellow Arts Council member Irene's, which I had not known about prior to the Arts Council meeting. Irene is a dainty little person who is a very kindly infant schoolteacher. She had said nothing about it being her birthday, either.

So it was a surprise to enter the Mandala Restaurant in Westport's main street after the meeting to find several tables pushed together and set up for a celebration of some kind.

There were also two gaily wrapped parcels at the far end of the table.

"Looks like there's going to be a party here tonight," I commented.

"Yes, silly, for you and Irene," Jan said, smiling her cheeky smile.

I knew then that she, Jan, had been the instigator.

We had barely been seated at the table when I asked, in child-like fashion: "please may we open our presents now?"

No, I was told, not for a little while. I was curious over the shape of the parcels and could hardly contain myself. Finally Jan, with a very cheeky grin said that yes, we could open our gifts. Irene quickly opened hers - a whoopee cushion. She is such a dainty person it seemed the most unlikely sort of gift to give her...

and I assumed that's the very reason why they gave it to her. My gift looked like a balloon. Why would they bother to wrap a balloon, I thought, unless it had a really funny slogan on it?

I slowly unwrapped it...a plain balloon, I thought as I peeled back the paper and looked for the funny slogan.

There was none. They had blown up a condom to give me and I'm sure my face must have been a study when I realized what the 'balloon' actually was. Not sure whether to feel insulted or amused, I nevertheless took the 'balloon' home and put it on the table. A slight breeze wafted it onto the floor and Reilly eyed it with deep suspicion. The concept of a balloon was an entirely new one to him and should be treated with great suspicion until it was proven safe. I casually observed Reilly over the next few days to see what his reaction would be to the balloon. On the first day he eyed it with suspicion and stuck his nose up close to it; he was taken aback when the 'thing' he could actually see through moved. The second day he gave it a couple of gentle pats and nosed it around the floor. He did the same thing over the next few days and then finally one day he sat back on his well-rounded haunches, lowered his head and gave a sniff at the balloon.

Then....lifting his front paw and bending his front leg back like an arm he gave the balloon an almighty wallop....and there was an instant bang. Reilly shot straight up in the air with fright and I almost cried with laughter.

Reilly landed back on the floor and glared at the horrible little bit of rubber that used to be the 'balloon'. Then, while I was still laughing, he gave an aloof look.

"About time I got rid of that thing! What's a single Christian woman like you doing with a thing like that on your floor, anyway?"

"For your entertainment only, dear boy!" I laughed.

"The frivolity's over, woman!"

"Great while it lasted though, eh?"

"If you say so."

He turned away with an aloof air, but not before I had seen the tell-tale gleam of mischief in his eyes.

**

One of Reilly's favourite games was to chirrup and race into my bedroom to get under my bed where he would promptly turn over on his back and with claws embedded in the underside of the bed base, would 'run' around underneath. Woe betide me if I dared to put my hand over the side!

I had been experiencing severe back pain for months. Going for walks, exercising at home, soaks in the bath - nothing seemed to ease it for long so finally I decided that it might be a good idea to buy a new bed and base. Which I did. And with some medical treatment plus the new bed, my back pain diminished dramatically.

But did Reilly care one way or the other? Oh yes! He was thoroughly put out when he discovered that he couldn't fit under the new base as it was a lot lower. Besides, Reilly had grown somewhat larger.

I say it was totally out of spite that he discovered he could have almost as much fun running around the *outside* of the base, pulling threads as he went. I was not amused. Sometimes I thought the sound of Reilly's claws going into the fabric and making a 'thwock, thwock' sound as he drew them out was a sure way of gaining my attention - and he sure got that! The rest of the time I'm sure he did it for the sheer hell of it, like leaping to the highest point of my drapes.

**

"I'd like to see Reilly in the water," said my nephew Greg, who was on holiday from school. My sister Sandy, her husband John and two of their three boys, Greg and Brett, visited for several days. They all lived in Christchurch, including their eldest son Lance, and some years before they had lived on the Coast. It was a chance for them to revisit walkways and other attractions during the May school holidays.

One of the attractions was in seeing Reilly swimming. I had told them about his adventures and they were intrigued. Off we went for a walk to the beach. Even the fact that Reilly walked with us intrigued them. At the beach he gave an excellent display of cavorting in the sand and on the driftwood.

Swimming was a different matter.

"It may be too cold for him," I warned. "Or then again he may simply decide he doesn't want to go for a swim."

There was a cold wind coming up the beach, and bringing sand with it. Gulls wheeled aloft, just a short distance over our heads. Reilly looked up at them, with one eye closing slightly, as if gauging the distance he could leap to catch one of them. He turned his head back to us and appeared to be cold. The wind rippled through his dense fur, showing the white underneath.

Reilly *didn't* want to go for a swim. He did, however, paddle around in the shallows and gallop over the wet sand, to finally sit on it and have a quick, inefficient wash.

"I didn't *intend* giving myself a good wash. I just wanted to show you guys how a cat doesn't mind sitting on wet sand - not like you humans! You like your home comforts."

"And I suppose you don't?" I said quietly.

"Of course I do! By the way, I didn't feel like a swim today... the water's too cold."

"I thought you were a big tough cat?" I asked, tongue in cheek, and earned some sidelong glances from family members.

Reilly gave me one of his haughty looks. That question was apparently too beneath him to answer.

Although Reilly hadn't actually gone swimming, my sister and her family were nevertheless fascinated by the quaint little things he demonstrated that day, and in fairness to Reilly, I wouldn't have wanted to go for a swim that day either! Perhaps if I had, Reilly would have come in with me, thinking that if it's okay for Mum to go for a swim, then it must also be okay for him.

**

While still living in Martin Place, friends asked me if I'd look after their cat Arnold, a pretty little female orange tabby. She had been named Arnold as my friends initially though she was a 'he', and anyway the name seemed to suit her, so they stuck with it even after they had discovered that Arnold was in fact, a girl cat. She was an independent little thing and as my friends were going out of town for a weekend, I said I'd pick up Arnold from town and bring her home.

"Won't Reilly mind?" they asked.

"I've got a strong feeling he'll enjoy the company and since Arnold's a girl there shouldn't be any rivalry problems," I replied.

And indeed that is the way it was. Arnold liked to explore and although I was concerned she might explore too far, she stayed within the near vicinity and enjoyed the large playing area and new sights and sounds.

One night, a few nights before I picked up Arnold from my friends' house, Reilly had got up on the roof at two o'clock and thundered up and down. There was to be no more sleep for me for a while, even though I put a pillow over my head and tried to sleep under that. The thundering went on. Exasperated, I got out of bed and went outside. With a furtive look around to make sure no one was watching, I climbed the tree from where Reilly had leaped, and retrieved him. I hoped no one had seen me. It is not considered the usual thing to do - to climb, in one's white nightshirt, up a tree at two o'clock in the morning!

When I fetched Arnold a few days later, I'm sure she and Reilly must have had a conversation which could have gone like this:

Arnold: "What's she like, really?"
Reilly: "She's all right. Needs sorting out every so often, though."
Arnold: "How often?"
Reilly: "Every day! Try her on the roof-thundering. I like to see her face. It really makes her mad."
Arnold: "Why do *that?*"
Reilly (loftily): "What do *you* think? She can't sleep! It's just another one of my ways to get back at people!"
Arnold: "That's not very nice."
Reilly: "But I'm cute all the same, huh? Huh?"
Arnold: "And a big-head. But I kinda like you."

Fortunately, when Arnold decided to try something of the same, it wasn't too late at night. I'd gone to bed to read for a while and had decided that when I was ready to put the light out, I'd call the cats inside. I hadn't been reading for long when the thundering began, but this time it was a lighter sound.

"Arnold!" I said out loud. "I hope she can get back down."

Up and down the roof she went. I couldn't see Reilly anywhere, but there was no doubt he was the instigator of this game, and it was quite possible he was looking on, from a strategic point that I couldn't see, and smirking. I could feel my temper rising. I got out of bed and went outside in my nightshirt. There didn't seem to be anyone around to see me. After coaxing Arnold back off the roof and while on my way back down the tree I heard a loud: "ahem! A nice night it is too, for climbing trees!"

"Sure is!" I said as cheerfully as I could muster under the circumstances.

The young couple who'd come around the corner on their evening walk said they were intrigued to see this person in her nightshirt, up a tree.

"My broomstick isn't running so well," I quipped. "I thought it was safer to go this way."

They stayed chatting for a while and I must say it was a most pleasant time. Just before I left the district they told me that a woman who, clad in her nightshirt, would think nothing of climbing up a tree to rescue a cat, would be a very interesting person to get to know. I was pleased and flattered. It isn't many people who understand, I said. We've been friends ever since.

**

My friends Kevin and Shelley, who were Arnold's owners brought their cute little cross-bred nut brown dog Inky to visit. Inky had personality-plus and was most interested in Reilly, who began stalking him.

"What a big brown rat. Biggest I've seen, I have to admit. Hey rat, dis is a showdown kid, and do you know who's gonna win? ME!"

"Get that look out of your eyes, Reilly, and leave Inky alone. He just wants to play," I said.

"Huh, me *play* with a big fat rat? You've gotta be joking!"

"Reilly!" I warned, as he slunk closer.

"Your eyesight needs checking out, fat cat. I am not a rat, but a fine, upstanding hero of a dog who would defend his humans to the last and who is also an excellent possum hunter."

"Possum hunter you may be, but I still say you're a rat."

"And I still say you need your eyes tested!"

"Wanna come test them, rat?"

Reilly slunk even closer.

Inky did a little excited dance and whined, unsure of what Reilly was going to do next. Reilly made a feint and Inky leaped back. He sank onto his haunches and tried to outstare the big cat.

"I can outstare you any day, rat."

"*I* don't need to prove myself. I *know* what I am!"

"Yeah, a big brown rat."

"I'm a fine big dog. Is your hearing bad as well?"

"Youse on my territory, buster. Do I remove you in my lightning fast way or will you go quietly? Scuttle, scuttle, rat!"

Inky whined again and trotted back for consolation with my friends. He backed into the safety of their 'fold' and kept a close watch on the dreadful cat who had insulted him.

"This is better than watching television!" Shelley laughed.

And so it was. Like a couple of boxers, each trying to out-maneuver the other without laying a hand (or paw) on each other, Reilly and Inky did a ritual dance of strangers assessing each other's capabilities.

Inky finally gave a snort and sat down with his nose on his paws, ears alert, but pretending nonchalance.

"Your day will come, rat." Reilly sat back and began to wash himself, - he too, apparently nonchalant. Inky gave a disinterested snort and yawned. We all laughed.

"I really don't see why I should have to lower myself to your level, fat cat."

"Think of yourself as being elevated to a prestigious position, brown rat."

"Must I remind you that I am not a brown rat, but a great hero of a dog? Anyway, what position?"

"The prestigious position of being in my presence."

"What an *ego!*"

"Hiss, growl, brown rat!"

"Bark, bark, fat, egotistical cat!"

"Dis is *my* territory!"

"*You* are an inhospitable, egotistical, fat cat!"

"I heard you the first time, rat. You keep behind *your* human, and I'll...well...sort of keep behind mine. Anyway, I'm not fat... that's all muscle!"

"Bark, bark!"

"Hiss, spit!"

The entertainment that evening was indeed better than what we saw on television.

**

REILLY — CUPBOARD-LOVER

"PLAYING? ...AM NOT!!"

CHAPTER NINE

Neighbourly Love

On many mornings after I'd let Reilly out early and had gone back to sleep, I was woken by the neighbour's corgi Gwyn. Gwyn lived on the other side of where Pepsi lived and set up a constant yapping of frustration. Many times I had wondered why little Gwyn should bark like that, particularly at that early hour of the morning.

It was some time before I found out the reason - I should have known it would have something to do with Reilly. He would, as neighbour Eileen said, bait Gwyn by sitting on top of the high wooden fence and staring down at her - or put his paw under the fence and bat it back and forth until Gwyn, in a frenzy, would leap for the paw which would promptly disappear. Even if Reilly had *not* removed his paw, no doubt Gwyn would have come off worst by far. Sometimes Reilly acted as if he was slow and ponderous, but to those animals who didn't know him, this was one of his ploys. Which they soon discovered to their detriment.

**

It was time to collect more wood from the beach. Gathering a few plastic bags to take with me, I asked Reilly: "wanna come to the beach?"

He chirruped as I donned my little red gumboots, and off we went outside. I unlocked the car door and in Reilly leaped to his favourite place in the back. As usual, I felt immense pride in taking him in my car and it was clear that he felt the same way... that is, proud to be seen out and about in my car.

At the beach, I let him out, grabbed some bags and locked the car. Reilly chirruped again as he raced off down the sandy laneway, his tail frisking from side to side. What joy I felt in *his* delight. It truly was an experience of so enjoying the *now* that it still pulls at my heartstrings when I recall the moments.

I began to collect wood, stopping every so often to breathe in deeply the salt-laden air. It was tangy and sweet on the breeze. Reilly enjoyed the air too, holding his head up, his nose twitching with pleasure. I wandered further down the beach and looked up to see a young woman approaching with a medium-sized spotted dog following her. The woman was from the health department and had come to the beach to take water samples. The dog looked friendly and seemed keen to make friends with Reilly as well.

"Is that *your* dog?" I asked, having seen the dog on several other occasions and wondered to whom he belonged.

"Oh no. He just followed me down here."

"Nice dog," I said, and just then Reilly, who had been circling the dog, leaped at him. The dog ran away, whining, with Reilly in full pursuit.

"That wasn't very nice!" I exclaimed. "My cat has such bad manners!"

The young woman laughed. "That really looked funny! It's usually the other way round! It's almost like watching a film clip in reverse!" She took her leave, chuckling, and went on down to the sea to collect her water samples.

Reilly returned after a minute or so and had a smug look.

"That dog was only trying to be friendly," I said sternly.

"Thought you wanted a tough tomcat?"

"I did, but not as tough as *you!*"

"You got what you prayed for, woman. Just be thankful I'm not a wimp."

"A wimp you certainly *aren't*," I agreed, sighing.

**

Over a period of several months, Pepsi the neighbour's cat and Reilly seemed to have come to an understanding, shaky though it was.

Reilly: "You stick to your place and I'll visit when I like."

Pepsi: "Hiss. You males are an arrogant lot! What a cheek, saying you will visit when you like! I would have to *invite* you first!"

Reilly: "Who do you think *you* are?"

Pepsi: "An emancipated cat."

Reilly: "Huh. An emancipated *pig* is more likely! *I've* seen the way you scoff your food!"

Pepsi: "Nonsense. I'm a dainty eater. Ask my humans."

Reilly: "Whatever you say, emancipated pig."

Pepsi: "Cat."

Reilly: "Or whatever. Anyway, as I was saying, you stick to your place and I'll visit when I want."

Pepsi: "Selfish, arrogant beast."

Reilly: "*King* of the beasts, that's me!"

Pepsi: "Of all the cats there are in the neighbourhood, why did I have to be landed with *you* for a neighbour?"

Reilly: "'Cos you're a very lucky, emancipated cat!"

Reilly was looking smug again.

Pepsi looked proud and queenly.

Pepsi: "Oo yes indeed! I *am*, aren't I?"

Reilly: "Oo yes indeed! You *are* a lucky cat!"

Reilly went around the corner of the house and snickered. It's *true!* I *heard* him!

Although Reilly and Pepsi weren't always civil to one another, I'll always have a soft spot for Pepsi. It was she who caught a field mouse soon after I'd moved next door and wanted to show it to me. Having no further interest in the mouse, I concluded that Pepsi had caught it especially for *my* sake, knowing I was lonely. Reilly had not arrived on the scene, at that stage, and my evenings were often very quiet.

The field mouse was in shock so I put him in an ice cream container filled with shredded paper, and added small pieces of grain bread for him to chew on when he'd recovered, plus I'd added a tiny lid with some water in it. I put the ice cream container near the fireplace (but not *too* close!) and carried on with my writing work. About a couple of hours later I heard a scuffling sound and out the mouse popped and eyed me quizzically. He sat, seemingly unafraid, in the middle of the lounge floor and preened his whiskers - the action delightful and so dainty. I was fascinated. *What a perfect little creature*, I thought. I moved closer to the little fellow and off he scampered, behind the sofa, up the back of a drape or under the table. It took me a while to realize that he was playing hide and seek with me. It didn't seem possible, but each time I had attempted to get close to him, he would run away, then pop back out in the middle of the lounge floor and calmly preen himself again in front of me. Some hours later I had the feeling he wanted to leave and so I opened the ranchslider door and watched the light shimmering of the drape as he scuttled along behind it and shot outside.

It was thanks to that little mouse that I was saved from having a lonely evening, and thanks also to Pepsi for bringing him to me. On a later evening it was a baby hedgehog calmly crunching at a malt biscuit held in my hand, who gave me a delightful evening.

A matter of just a few weeks later and my life was turned upside down with the arrival of Reilly.

**

Freelance writing opportunities became more and more scarce as circumstances changed, and I already had a backlog of rural stories written and sent which would probably take months before they all went to print - even if I'd stopped working right then. Alas, one rural, South Island-wide newspaper practically filled their next edition with my stories. So that meant writing some more, also the type of stories with a reasonable 'shelf-life'.

After I had completed those and sent them away, I took on other jobs, such as tutoring a twenty-hour course in creative writing, compiling the District Council, initially quarterly, then later thrice-yearly newspaper and doing on-call newspaper work as well as continuing with writing my rural stories. But the writing - no pun intended - was on the wall. I figured I was able to stay on for about another few months, but no more. On occasional trips away I would do reporting work but that simply meant my backlog was increasing. Additionally, I had to go further away to interview people and one interview could mean being away for the complete day.

Lou rang me one day to say a job for an advertising features writer had been advertised in the Nelson Evening Mail. Would I be interested? I wasn't sure. I had thought that maybe I could stay in the district for up to another year, providing I took on part time work not associated with writing. But even part time jobs were not easy to come by. I thought seriously about the newspaper job over the next few days and then applied. A few days after that I received a call to say I had been short listed for the job and would I go for an interview in Nelson? I agreed, although my heart sank. Could I do fulltime work again to set hours? Looking at my dwindling bank balance after I had paid for my car registration and a few other big bills I knew that there was no alternative. I was already doing full time work, but at least I wasn't bound by office hours. I could work until midnight if I wanted to, and take the next morning off. Provided I had met all deadlines, I was pretty much my own boss, which was an ideal lifestyle.

I debated with myself, over and over, if this move was a good one. Somehow I felt the tug to go, even though my heart wasn't in it. It was as if I was *meant* to go, for reasons unknown at the time.

I went for the interview in Nelson, with the strong feeling I'd be employed – but better still, possibly at a small branch in Motueka where there would be just three of us working, with others popping in from time to time. I returned to the Coast and told Reilly that I was sure I would get the job and did he mind shifting?

"Nope. A change is as good as a rest."

"I hope you're sure. Because this shift will be for several months at least!"

"Wherever you go, I go - that's what a good cat I am, I am."

"Oh Reilly, I'm glad you understand!" I said, my heart overflowing, and stroked him tenderly.

"No need to go all mushy on me, woman."

"That's the way I feel. We've got dramatic changes coming up, puss."

"Yeah, well."

"Is that all you've got to say?"

"Yeah, well."

I got up from the sofa, my mind furiously busy. Would I take the job or not? I had the feeling that it would not be the initial advertised job for an advertising feature writer, and it wasn't. In the end I did take the job, as editor of the Motueka Sun, but with a pay increase on what they'd first suggested. I'd told the pleasant young woman secretary over the telephone that there was no point in my going to all the trouble of moving out of the district to a job that was only paying the same as I was already getting from my freelance work, and she agreed. She rang me the next day to say that the increase had been agreed with and when could I start? I named the date - four weeks away, and stuck with it despite protests. Finalizing other writing commitments, giving notice on the property I rented, organizing a removal truck and the many other tasks that no one else could do for me could not be done in just a few days.

Reilly prowled around the house in the days before we left, both restless and curious as I cleaned and re-scrubbed the house that never seemed to look clean no matter how hard I tried. I told Reilly about the forthcoming trip, reminding him about how much he enjoyed rides in the car. Naughty as Reilly could be, his behaviour in the car was almost astounding - he enjoyed rides so much and was so well behaved.

My friend Keith and his son Tony, and Tony's friend moved the majority of heavy furniture out the night before moving day and at nine o'clock that night I was lying exhausted in the bath when there was a knock at the door.

"Who is it?" I called.

It was Richard and Lorna, the friends who'd first seen me coming down out of a tree after rescuing Arnold the cat. I called out that I wouldn't be long and quickly dried myself off and got dressed.

"We saw the piece in Rowel's Column about you leaving and thought we'd better come to say goodbye," they said as I opened the door to them.

Rowel's Weekend Roundup in Friday's local newspaper was that: a roundup of mainly amusing, but also controversial events over the past week. I came in a category outside of 'controversial', I like to think.

We had to sit on cushions on the floor as the lounge suite was already stowed away on the locked truck outside. We drank coffee, told stories and generally had an amusing time. They left after midnight and I couldn't sleep for a while, I was so overtired.

After about two hours' sleep I got up at five o'clock to do more packing. Oh why did I hoard so much? But you could guarantee that after I'd thrown something out after having saved it 'just in case' for maybe five or more years, the very next day after having finally thrown it out it would come in handy.

Murphy's Law, or the Law of Cussedness. *Maybe Reilly should have been named Murphy,* I thought.

After Keith and the boys had driven off in the truck full of my furniture, there still seemed to be cleaning and other bits and pieces to sort out. Nearly an hour later I still hadn't finished.

There was a gentle knock at the door. It was Eileen, Gwyn's 'mother'. She asked me if I would have time for a cup of tea and much as I longed for one, I had to say no. She looked so disappointed I felt awful. I explained that the truck was already an hour ahead of me and that maybe one other day we could have a cup of tea together.

"I'll hold you to that," she warned.

"Does that mean Reilly can come too?"

"Oh, that dreadful cat of yours! I'm sure he could find something to amuse himself with - baiting Gwyn, no doubt!"

I laughed tiredly and Eileen left. I felt very sad. I had been getting to know her well and enjoyed her sharp wit. I promised myself that I would indeed have that cup of tea with her one day. And I did.

I loaded my vacuum cleaner and other cleaning bits and pieces into my car, put Reilly in his cage and put him on the front seat: he was too excited to be alarmed. And off we went, stopping just up the road to drop the house key off at a friend's place, and then continued our journey. I was filled with misgivings: I knew the job wasn't what I would like and I also felt it wouldn't last long even though it was intended to be a permanent position.

But in the meantime I decided not to dwell on the might or might not be's, and concentrated on enjoying the beautiful early spring scenery.

**

CHAPTER TEN

A New Beginning

The house I began renting in Motueka was only seven years old. Light, airy and fresh, it was a joy to live in after the previous house which had no insulation and was in a poor state of repair.

Reilly and I gradually settled in to living in the two-storeyed home. He enjoyed running up and down the stairs, his plump fluffy rear wobbling as he chirruped and ran. The decking outside the top storey was also a joy to him. He pounded up and down the timber flooring, relishing the echoing drum of his running, and he also liked to leap onto the railing. I would watch him, my heart in my mouth, and think of the times I'd read about cats falling from a great height. They didn't *always* land upright. Reilly, sensing my unease, would glare at me haughtily.

"Have you no faith in me, woman?"

I would turn away and go about my business, not daring to watch any further. With all his leaping and general acrobatics, Reilly rarely mistimed his landings.

He liked Motueka but I felt I could never take him to the beach there. Why? I have no idea except to put it down to instinct. Hooligans lurking, a dangerous rip in the tide, perhaps? It was a shame in a way, because of an evening the beach was practically deserted and quite lovely. And so was the car parking area with its majestic trees and landscaped picnic grounds.

I sensed Reilly's creeping boredom. He assuaged it by getting into the neighbour's market garden, exploring in the kiwifruit orchard over the back of the property I was renting - sending off neighbouring cats who dared to wander onto what Reilly had already (in the first few days) claimed as his own territory, running over the tiled roof of the modern block of flats next door (and incurring the wrath of one of the owners, I later heard), and catching birds.

The lounge and dining rooms were directly above the carport, and as the lining of the carport ceiling had not been completed, birds found their way through gaps in the building paper. A number of birds made their nests in there and the din at times was deafening. When the birds were moving around inside the building paper, upstairs, Reilly would cavort from spot to spot on the lounge or dining room floor, wherever he deemed the birds would be underneath. It was most entertaining. But since he couldn't see anything, after a while he would grow bored and leap onto the dining room window sill to stare at the starlings in the silver beech tree swaying in the breeze.

"I'm gonna catch one of them birds soon, woman."

"Nothing would surprise me about you," I said. "But just remember that starlings are pretty smart birds."

Reilly ignored me as if I hadn't spoken and continued to stare at the birds.

It wasn't long before I had the unpleasant task of burying several starlings and a blackbird. Some of the babies fell out of their nests in the roof and these Reilly snapped up with relish, and growled when I neared him. I tried to feel dispassionate about the whole scene but it wasn't easy. However, saying aloud: "Oh well, that's nature" always helped keep things in perspective, even though I still felt sad at the loss.

Reilly became restless and moody. I just knew he missed going to the beach but even after several months I still felt it was important not to take him.

"I can't take this much longer, y'know."

"I know, I know. Never mind Reilly, we'll be going back to the Coast soon and you can go to the beach as much as you like."

"Just as well."

Reilly was still moody. I put it down to loneliness as well as boredom.

"I think you need your very *own* cat," I told him one day, after observing his boredom. His ears pricked up but I said no more about it at that stage.

Just before Christmas I returned to the Coast, taking Reilly to the Four Foot Lodge Cattery and animal shelter on the way. He seemed to enjoy his little holiday away. On my return from a further trip to the Coast I heard other cats in the near vicinity and asked about them. I was told about a dear little cat, very young, which had been brought in with her litter. Her kittens were chosen, but she was left behind. Once I'd held her and gazed into her enormous green eyes I was sunk. She was so grateful in being cuddled and I delighted in her loving nature. How could *anyone* abandon a beautiful little cat like this, I wondered.

The cat was only about ten months old, underweight, and with scratches and bites from the other cats. It was a miracle, I felt, that her nature was still so loving and gentle.

I took Reilly home and thought and thought about the little cat at the animal shelter, for the rest of the week. I talked to Reilly about it. Then late on a Saturday afternoon in January I rang the lodge. Did they still have that dear little dark tabby female cat, which actually seemed to be part Oriental? Yes they did, came the reply.

"Can I have her?" I asked, feeling a rush of love for the little cat. "She's been on my mind ever since I saw her."

I was told I could have her and, excited, I told Reilly then off I rushed, taking Reilly's cage with me. Reilly looked nonchalant, but I knew he was as excited as what I was.

When I reached the lodge I told the very nice lady there - also named Lois - that I had already decided on a name for the little cat.

"She is Katie O'Brien," I said. The name seemed so right for her, and it drew a smile from Lois.

Katie O'Brien was frightened of the car; no doubt she recalled past experiences. She messed herself with fright. Back at home, I took her into the laundry, closed the sliding door and let her out of the cage. She sat in a cool spot under the stairs and quietly observed me as I gently talked to her while cleaning out the cage. I felt it was important to do the cleaning in that order: the cage first and then her.

Then I slowly began the process of cleaning her up.

She was very dirty, not just with her own excrement, but also with the grime of many weeks. Her gratitude was enormous when the gentle cleaning was done.

With many cuddles and quiet chats, I took her outside and lay on the back lawn with her. It was a wonderful time of bonding. I had been told to keep her inside for a week but knew instinctively that I wouldn't need to. And I didn't. That important bonding we had at that time established our house as her house too, Reilly as a sort of permanent fixture and I as her human.

It was lovely out there on the lawn in the early evening. Reilly was enchanted with the little black smoke and tabby female - no rivalry there! As I studied her, her name seemed firmly entrenched. It seemed to suit her waif-like appearance, with her dainty black smoke body with dark tabby markings and green eyes too big for her delicate face. Again I wondered how on earth anyone could leave behind such a dear little cat. She was so filled with love and gratitude it was almost overwhelming.

When Reilly drew closer to inspect her she gave a warning chatter. He sat back, not at all put out, and rolled over on his back to play, and also to let her know he was no threat. Good. It showed he was relaxed with her, but I warned Katie not to get too close to him, because that beautiful, fluffy silver grey and white body held a tiger in disguise.

But Katie had already guessed that.

She might have looked waif-like, but she was smart. I guess that having to share a big cage with a number of other cats - one of them cunningly vicious - soon had her 'street-wise'.

There was little sleep for me that night. Reilly slept in the spare bedroom and Katie slept with me. That is, she slept on and off. Every twenty minutes or so she came up to my face, purring loudly to let me know how grateful she was.

And just as Reilly did, she too, ate and ate solidly for two months, afraid that each meal was to be her last.

A month later, when she was looking far healthier, she was spayed. When I came to pick up Katie after her operation, one of the vet nurses said she was intrigued by her name.

"I thought I was the only one who wanted to give their cat two names," she said with a smile. "My cat's name is Tommy Slater."

I told her that I thought it was a wonderful name.

As it happened, Katie had also had intestinal worms, and the vet nurse said it came in handy for training purposes, so their trainees could see exactly what worms looked like. The nurse said that they often had new cats, left behind in catteries as the owners didn't want them any more, being brought into their consulting rooms. Those cats always needed worming.

"I can't imagine why anyone would want to leave their cat behind, but there's no explaining why humans behave the way they do at times," she said sadly. "But your Katie O'Brien! She's such a dear little soul! You must be so happy with her!"

I told the nurse that I was, and so was my other cat. We discussed the merits of cats for a few minutes longer and then I left, feeling as if I had made a new friend in the vet nurse. Back home, Katie sat neatly on the rug and rested. Reilly came near to investigate the medical smell about her. Chattering, she told him to keep his distance. He did. I was amazed at Reilly's attitude. He appeared to actually respect her! Alas, it did not last long. When she had recovered, he assumed his bullying ways and as so often was the case, I had to dash to the rescue when Katie set up her plaintive 'piping'.

All the same, given his chauvinistic nature, Reilly did seem to be fond of his little friend and his boredom was eased considerably. He allowed Katie, for short spells at a time, to wash him and one day I saw him return the favour. But when he saw me watching him he immediately stopped and looked out the window as if nothing had happened.

It was obvious he did not want to be *seen* to be caring!

**

I was fascinated with my cats' similar colouring. Katie had an Oriental look about her, and with her daintiness and the way she wanted to leap from the floor to my chest or on my back (very disconcerting at times!) led me to becoming convinced she indeed had Oriental breeding somewhere in her ancestry.

I've already established that Reilly is no ordinary cat, but what *breed* of cat he was, I was unsure. I borrowed a book from the Motueka District Library. The book was an extensive study of more than 250 breeds of cats and their origins and ancestry. Both of my cats had that wonderful fur, when in a breeze, it took on a 'smoke' effect. I decided after studying the many photographs and text on colours, build and habits, that Reilly was a Norwegian Forest Cat and Katie an Oriental black smoke. Which you could say puts paid to their Irish names. I choose now to ignore their heritage and supplant it with my own!

"Why do your cats have Irish names?" someone asked me.

"Because they meow with an Irish accent," I replied, straight-faced.

"Really? Well, I've never heard of *that* before!" the person had said seriously. "How does it sound?"

"Like a kind of 'meow-rrr', as said with an Irish brogue," I replied, trying not to grin.

I repeated the conversation to our church minister who laughingly told me I was daft.

I laughed. "I love being daft and anyway God made me this way!"

The minister chuckled. "Indeed He did."

**

One day I arrived home late after an exhausting trip to Golden Bay for reporting purposes. By that time my other newspaper job had fizzled out (which I had strongly suspected it would, from the very day I drove up to Motueka for my big move there) when a big newspaper company had taken over, and I had simply continued my freelance writing for rural newspapers. The particular trip I had made that day had involved reporting for three rural South Island-wide and nationwide newspapers and what a long day it was.

My cats were pleased to see me and after feeding them I was about to start on a meal when there was a knock at the ranchslider door. It was the market gardener from next door, visiting to show me plans for the unit he intended building.

He seemed to have something else on his mind, and then out it came, rather bluntly. He said he didn't care for cats, that they were a nuisance and had often dug up his young plants. "Well, I'm going to be open and honest with you," he said fervently.

"Please do," I said, trying to hide a smile, but all the same, wondering what sort of calamitous information he was going to part with.

"I've made a trap for the cats around here!"

"A trap?" I echoed, aghast. "I do hope it won't *hurt* them!"

When I expounded my very strong views on the cruelty of gin traps he replied hastily that no, it was nothing like that.

"I just want to give them a fright to deter them off the property. Once they get in the cage I turn the hose on them. That soon sorts them out!"

I dared to ask him if Reilly had been one of the culprits.

"Yes, your big cat was one of them too! And he'll get hosed again if he gets caught."

"Fair enough," I said. "I'm glad you told me." I hid a smile, although I still didn't care for his attitude towards cats.

After he'd left, Reilly returned to the room, smirking.

"What are you smirking at?"

"I *saw* him and *heard* him! Did he think he'd given me a fright?"

"I think that was the idea," I answered.

"Did you tell him I love water?"

"Of course not," I grinned.

We both stood there smirking, of one accord.

**

Just before our newspaper closed, there had been a few weeks when we would come to work and notice that computer gear was missing. At first I thought we'd had burglars, and was going to telephone the police, but it transpired through a few discreet enquiries that the managing editor and her husband had not seen fit to tell their staff that they were gradually moving their gear to Nelson. It was a most cavalier attitude and sometimes I wished that I *had* phoned the police! That would have given the owners something to think about: that it is a miserable thing to do, to start removing computers and whatnot from an office without saying anything to their staff members. This was in preparation to what the managing editor eventually said was a merger with the Nelson newspaper, but at the big re-launch party in one of the local hotels I was secretly pleased when the gung-ho manager of the big newspaper group stated emphatically, following the managing editor's syrupy speech about the merger, that it was *not* a merger; that it was actually a complete *takeover!* I took grim pleasure in seeing the embarrassment on the former managing editor's face.

I met one of the regular newspaper advertisers there. He was, quite frankly a lecherous man and I discovered later that he had a bad reputation for hounding single women. He made some insinuations to me which I brushed off at the time. What I didn't know is that he had been making enquiries about me and discovered where I lived.

One morning on a Sunday there was a loud banging on the downstairs door. I couldn't think who would be visiting me at this early hour and on a Sunday, too. I went down the stairs to the door which unfortunately, was clear glass and as such, did not have a peephole where I could see who was calling first. It was the lecherous man from the newspaper re-launch party, much to my dismay.

He cheerfully told me he'd been making enquiries about me and found out where I lived and could he come in? He wanted to spend time with me, he said.

"Oh yes?" I said, skeptically. "Does your wife know you're here?"

"She's out of town and anyway, this is about *us!*"

"There is no *us!*" I told him bluntly. "What made you think there would be?"

"You're good-looking and friendly, and I thought you might be up for it!" he told me breezily.

"You thought completely wrong!" I told him.

Reilly came thundering down the stairs. "What's going on?"

"I have an unwanted caller," I told Reilly as I looked down at him.

The man looked at me in puzzlement. "You mean you're not gonna invite me in for a little chat and a bit of slap and tickle?"

"If you don't go now, the only bit of slap you're going to get is across your face!"

Reilly lunged at him and sunk his teeth into his leg.

"Ow! Ow! Get this thing off me!" He shook his leg but Reilly clung to him. The man grabbed the door to regain his balance and at the same time, Reilly let go. The man fell into the doorway and swore.

"Fancy swearing at me too, and on a Sunday!" I stood there with my arms folded and waited for the man to get to his feet. He did and took a step towards me. Reilly flew at him again, this time hissing and biting.

"I'm getting out of here!" the man shouted. "I was told that reporters can be dangerous and it's the truth! You mark my words, I'll let the news get around that it's true!" He limped away and Reilly spat out a bit of cloth from the man's trouser leg.

"Actually, it's my cat who's even more dangerous than me!" I called after the man had got to his feet and moved away. "Don't come back or else I'll phone your wife when she gets back, that's if she *was* even away!"

"Pah!" Reilly spat. "I could have been *poisoned* by dat man! He tasted *terrible!*"

"Thank you for coming to support me, Reilly. I really do appreciate you!" I picked him up for a cuddle.

"Arrgh! You soppy woman! Put me down so I can spit out da rest of dis tacky stuff."

I put him down with a smile.

"Now, I wonder how he's gonna explain the strange chunk of cloth out of his pants and the bite on his leg?" Reilly added, while still spitting out little bits of cloth.

"No doubt he'll have some excuse," I said. "Anyway, I highly doubt he'll be back. You are such a good watch cat!"

"Yes I am, aren't I?" Reilly said smugly as he bounded back up the stairs, with me following.

**

I visited my friend Jewell, who lived in the hills at Mahana. Jewell is another animal lover and in the past we've had marvelous discussions on the antics of our animals. On this particular day Jewell gave me a cat mint plant to take home. She had cat mint growing everywhere and, reluctant to uproot and throw any of them away, she was only too happy for me to take one of her plants home.

I was delighted and so were the cats. I kept the plant on the high sideboard, with other things around it to give it a chance to flourish. Which it did. Occasionally I would shift the plant around a little and the cats, in turn, would wriggle and smooch around it. I would have to move the plant again, and how hard I tried to look after it!

It grew well, providing I kept it away from the cats.

But what's a cat mint plant there for, if not to provide pleasure for cats? Reilly nudged it and swooned around it and then one day lifted his front paw back in a sweeping gesture and *whang!* He knocked the top half clean off the plant. It looked funny, but that was the beginning of the end of my poor cat mint plant. I was disappointed but not surprised...well maybe just a little, in that the plant lasted for as long as it did before major intervention from Reilly.

"I *always* wanted to do that! What magnificent claws I have! What a swordsman I would make!"

"I deeply suspect you did it because you knew I liked that plant," I accused.

"Would I do that?"

"Yes you would."

"I am mortally wounded."

"You, a good swordsman, mortally wounded?" I shot back.

"I will not lower my dignity to reply to that crack."

He stalked off, clearly affronted, turning the tables on me yet again. How did he do it? After all, it was *I* who had been upset by the brutalizing of one of my favourite plants!

The person who once said that cats have an inbuilt cunning, developed and fine-tuned over thousands of years, sure said a mouthful.

It made the craftiest of human beings seem amateurs in comparison.

**

REILLY — ROTARY CAT-NAPPER.

"I LIKE TO SLEEP AROUND."

CHAPTER ELEVEN

A Gentle Romance

As far as I knew, Reilly had never had a romance. I had wondered, when we were still in Martin Place, at Carter's Beach in Westport if he'd had a bit of a crush on Pepsi, the way a younger man might have on an older woman. But if that was the case, Reilly never told me. I decided he was very cunning over his friendships, romantic or otherwise. He had been neutered, but that didn't always deter cats from at least 'having a go' as it were. Having seen a neutered cat enjoying a romance with a cat I'd had some years before, I can attest to romance not being dead and buried just because a cat has had a 'little operation'!

I had despaired at times over Reilly's behaviour; indeed it could be so bad I doubted if Reilly could possibly have *any* friends. They would have to be of the very compassionate, long suffering variety to put up with Reilly's arrogance, his sheer devilment and sarcasm, coupled with occasional sentiment, sweetness and adorability. Compassionate and long-suffering? Hey, that describes *me!*

Reilly did not always like to be seen to be caring, as I mentioned in the previous chapter, so it was a pleasure when I brought the waif-like Katie O'Brien home to hear Reilly chirruping *his* pleasure.

"Hey! My very own little cat! How nice! Actually, sometimes you're not too bad, woman."

Katie's chattering to keep Reilly at a distance served only to intrigue him all the more. Katie, small and dainty, but with an already-surfacing charm and individuality, represented a challenge Reilly could not possibly resist.

When my three sisters visited at Easter, they thought Katie was wonderful. She accepted their loving with gratitude and enormous pleasure. Much as my sisters admired Reilly, they soon became aware that inside his wonderful fluffy body of beautiful colouring was a feisty, eccentric cat. Our youngest sister Sandy had already seen him in action at Martin Place, and quickly warned the others about him.

Reilly didn't care. He liked the feeling of power it gave him to have we 'mere' humans wary of him. He strutted around the big modern house with a smirk. I do believe some of his sense of power came with the immediate realization that he was the only male in a house full of adoring females. Contrary to the possibility of feeling outnumbered, he exerted all the authority possible: he was a veritable lion with his pride.

That 'air' went out the window, so to speak, when we all prepared for bed. Coralie pumped up an air bed and as it had been over-pumped, she let some of the air out. It made a loud and very rude noise and Reilly flew up into the air with shock, incurring our mirth.

Coralie went to bed first. A great cat lover, she appeared gratified when both cats settled themselves around her. Reilly peeped at me over Coralie's hip as she lay on her side in bed, a lightly wicked smile hovering. It appeared that he bore no grudge for the loud noise emitted earlier from letting air out from the air bed. I could have felt 'put out' that my cats had deserted me, but rather, was more amused and pleased than anything else. It proved how hospitable they could be.

I like to think that at least *some* of Katie's good manners were rubbing off onto Reilly.

**

When my sister Sandy had visited with her family back in January when I was still in Carter's Beach, she had given me a brown catnip mouse she'd made for Reilly. When Katie eventually came to live with us, they both were ecstatic over that mouse! It was chewed, rolled on, tossed and caught, tossed and caught again and rolled over. Round and round the house they went with it, taking turns to chew and roll. Then they would leave the mouse about a meter in front of the doorway. Amazingly, the catnip mouse survived for some months, even when I had moved to Motueka.

I saw odd looks on most of the faces of the people who came to view the Motueka house, which was up for sale. Several times, people trod on the mouse and I saw them shudder; presumably they thought they had trodden on an 'unmentionable'.

When we moved back to Westport, the mouse came too, along with small yellow balls, other, worn-out catnip mice, fluffy toys - and a little rubber caterpillar with a gorgeous little face. The caterpillar squeaked when it was squeezed. It cost over six dollars and Reilly ignored it completely.

As favourite toys, the small, weighted yellow balls and the brown mouse won hands down. The carpet in the lounge at our new home, a cottage in Archer Place, was in bold browns, beiges and gold, very seventies-style. The brown mouse was almost invisible when lying on that carpet. The same thing happened. Visitors arrived, trod on the mouse and gave shudders of revulsion. Their faces were a study of embarrassment and amusement when I explained what they had trodden on.

If Reilly was in the vicinity, he would always walk away with a smirk: no doubt, still more of his 'paying back process' at work. As he's said before: "when opportunity knocks...."

**

That Easter in Motueka, our eldest sister Dawn was enchanted with Katie, and sat at the breakfast table with Katie on her back in her arms, being held like a baby. Katie looked up at Dawn with her huge green eyes. It was a lovely moment: huge green eyes looking lovingly up at huge blue, compassionate eyes. I will never forget it.

When my three sisters left, if I hadn't my cats to keep me company, I would have felt very lonely indeed. All of us have a very similar sense of humour and it was great to share the things that amused us. Katie and Reilly watched the car as it went slowly down the drive, my sisters waving until they were out of sight. I felt a sweeping loss wash over me, which my cats sensed, of course.

"I expect you realize I liked your sisters?"

"Coming from *you*, Reilly, that is a compliment indeed," I answered.

The cats went scampering off and I went back inside. I watched them from my upstairs bedroom window while they frolicked on the lawn, and some of my feeling of loneliness disappeared.

**

Watching my cats frolicking on the lawn gave a rebirth to the thought I'd had at numerous times: did Reilly have any romantic attachments? Somehow he seemed too proud, too independent and arrogant to allow himself the 'weakness' of caring for another cat. But as the old saying goes: to every rule there is an exception. I wondered if Katie O'Brien could be that exception.

Certainly she had the advantage of proximity, and she had engaging little ways and had a forgiving nature. I'm sure that any other cat would have walked away and left Reilly to his independence and pride.

As I stood there and watched, Reilly's bottom wriggled and he leaped at Katie, who screamed and ran up the outside stairway. She cried to come inside. Reilly was directly behind her and had that look of devilment in his eyes.

I let them both inside and told Reilly off for his behaviour. He ignored me - and stole over to Katie, his tail swishing and his eyes wide with delight.

"I'm in the mood to pick on someone. *You'll* do, Katie O'Brien. Grrr!"

"Leave me alone! I want to eat."

"You're always *eating*, you fat slug."

"I bet *you* did the same when you first came to live with our human."

"So what if I did? That was *then*. This is *now*, you greedy piggy."

"I was a slug before."

"Pig, slug, shlug, fat cat, whatever! I'm in the mood for picking and you're *it*, Katie O'Brien!"

She ignored him for a moment while she ate. Reilly sat near her, watching every movement, then gave her a swipe with his solid paw.

"*Eek!* You're a *beast!*"

Reilly looked at her through narrowed eyes.

"Handsome, too."

"And conceited."

"I'm allowed to be. That's my prerogative."

"*Very* conceited and not only that, you're a bully."

"Just as long as you know who's boss around here."

"Our human is."

"What? *Her?* You *crawler!*"

"We of the fairer sex must stick together."

"Two's company, eh? That suits me. I can remain abstract and observe with an unjaundiced eye."

"Does that mean your other eye is jaundiced?"

Reilly looked bored.

"Yeah, you're right. You females should stick together. You're *all* daft. My eyes are *not* jaundiced. They are a magnificent shade of gold."

"How do you know?"

"Because, you weeny cat, I look in our human's mirror regularly to ensure my whiskers are straight. It is then that I am amazed yet again by my sheer good looks, and the unusual gold shade of my eyes. Anyway, our human told me so as well."

"I thought you didn't take any notice of what she says?"

"I do when it suits me."

"I think you're dreadful."

"Yeah, a dreadful, adorable cat, that's me!"

"Why did I ever come to this household?"

"Because our human is a softy and you looked...well...like a waif with those big green eyes."

"Awww...do you think I'm beautiful?"

"I have to admit that we cats, as a rule are mostly magnificent. Some of us stand out more than others, of course. *I'm* one of those, naturally."

"You haven't answered my question, Reilly. Do you think I'm beautiful?"

He eyed her up and down, chirruped and walked around her, sniffing delicately. Katie was wary; was this to be another of his ploys - pretending to be sweet and affectionate, but then leaping to attack?

Reilly sat on the grass and nonchalantly began to wash himself. Katie fidgeted.

"Well?"

"Well what?"

"Do you think I'm beautiful?"

He stopped washing himself and encompassed her with his golden eyes.

"As a matter of fact I do, but don't let it go to your head!"

"Oh Reilly, that's the nicest thing you've ever said to me!"

"O'Reilly? Yeah, that's me, tough tomcat, but mostly Mr Nice Guy."

Katie rolled over on her back and wriggled and squirmed invitingly.

"Do you really think I'm beautiful or are you just saying that to make me happy?"

Reilly's eyes half-closed. She was too, too tempting by far!

"You really *are* beautiful. Didn't I already say that?"

Katie squirmed even more and Reilly walked around the corner. Truly, I *heard* what he next said!

"Yeah, you're almost as good-looking as me!"

Then came that distinctive snicker.

**

CHAPTER TWELVE

The Return Home

The desire to return to the Coast was strong. I decided to make the shift before winter set in and made the roads in the Motueka Valley too icy for safe travel. I rang the Westport newspaper office and placed an advertisement for a house wanted to rent. I had three answers; two unsuitable, but the third sounded promising. I rang back and said I'd travel down to have a look at the property.

The house was less than half the size of the place I was renting in Motueka, but since nothing else had been offered in response to my advertisement, I made a quick decision and accepted, paying two weeks' rent in advance.

I had already given thirty days' notice on the Motueka house and those thirty days soon went, filled with packing and final reporting and visiting opportunities.

The day of the shift dawned clear and sunny, with just a light crispness in the air. Already it was late April. I gave Katie O'Brien a sedative about an hour before leaving, and around three quarters of an hour after the very efficient removal men left, I left too, loaded up with my cats, my sewing machine, my word processor and camera gear. The drive was most pleasant. I had told the girl at Telecom that I wanted my new phone number in Westport to be connected at two p.m., which was around the time I expected to be there. I gave a smile of satisfaction when I drove up onto the lawn and stopped, to see it was just one minute to two o'clock.

There was to be no let-up in work! An hour before I'd left Motueka the editor of one rural newspaper rang to ask me if I'd cover a story which had to be received in Wellington by the following Monday. It was already Wednesday. I told the editor I was in the process of shifting and had she received my change of address card? Yes she had, and had thought she might still be able to catch me before I moved out.

I promised I would get the story to her on time and I did. How, I don't know, as I was desperately tired by the end of that day and the next. I worked the next day regardless.

If that hadn't been enough, I was in the new home for only around fifteen minutes when the telephone rang. It was another editor, this one based in Auckland, to tell me what features I had to write for the next publication, which was a nationwide rural magazine. This time I had a shorter deadline.

I blanked my mind off the thought of stories for the rest of the day - otherwise I would have felt overwhelmed with them.

Reilly and Katie settled in really well, quickly establishing their territory. The neighbour's big ginger cat, euphemistically named Misty, chased Reilly up the beautiful eucalyptus tree at the front of the property, and Reilly never forgave him, taking every opportunity he could get to cat-er-waul at Misty, and generally 'vent his spleen'. Misty decided that Katie was the lesser of the two evils and thoroughly picked on her one day. Katie's screams had me running and Misty left the scene hurriedly when he saw me coming.

"Every cat that's lived here has been picked on by Misty," my dear little neighbour on the other side told me.

That's why I say Misty is euphemistically named. There was nothing misty about him whatsoever!

At Queen's Birthday Weekend when my sister Sandy and her husband John were visiting, there was a terrible din out the front. I ran to see what was happening, knowing instinctively it was Misty and Reilly at loggerheads again. I visualized cats having to be taken to the vet to have nasty abscesses lanced, and was determined to prevent any possibility of wounds occurring.

But was it too late? There at the end of the curved driveway were many tufts of ginger fur - the most I'd ever seen off one cat. At the same time as I retrieved Reilly - with a tuft of ginger fur still stuck amusingly in his mouth - and Misty staggered around the fence to his own territory, Misty's owners backed their van out of their drive. They couldn't have helped but notice all the fur, none of which was Reilly's, but they never said anything to me. I almost felt ashamed. I say *almost* because I, too, had not quite forgiven Misty for the awful welcome he gave us. Two days after arriving, I quietly told Misty to go home as he'd been back on Reilly's new territory, growling and waiting his chance to attack. It was not my cats who were recipients of his nasty nature this time, but me. After walking behind Misty to ensure he went back under the fence, he spun around and slashed at my leg. When I showed Misty's owner he was astounded, then he recalled Misty doing a similar thing to their own children.

It took months for the scar on my leg to fade, so really, I was quite proud of Reilly avenging me.

However, bickering went on for months, but gradually eased as both came to a very grudging acceptance of 'things that cannot be changed have to be accepted'.

I did think Reilly was pretty cheeky though, when I'd spy him next door, yowling obscenities to Misty on Misty's own territory. The big ginger cat viewed Reilly with hate in his eyes.

When Misty returned to our side of the fence Reilly would yowl obscenities again. It seemed to me that a week never went by without Reilly having to express himself in a very uncouth and vocal manner.

Misty visited on numerous occasions: I always hoped Reilly was away sleeping somewhere. A sucker for any cat, I sometimes gave Misty a snack of tasty cat biscuits, which were demolished within a minute. Maybe the snacks helped to restore better relations between the cats; certainly by then Misty had decided, even though I was that dreadful new cat's *human*, maybe I wasn't so bad after all, and maybe he shouldn't have given me such a nasty swipe that day.

**

It was a beautiful early spring afternoon with the only sounds coming from the Cape Foulwind cement works trucks and a few other vehicles going by on the main road to the rear of my rented property.

As I wrote, I heard an odd rustling sound in the big eucalyptus tree, this particular one in the back yard. The rustling sound was caused by two fat native wood pigeons, known also by the Maori name of *kereru* (among other, similar names), hopping from branch to branch. The birds looked far too heavy to be supported by the branches. They sat there in all their plush magnificence, white aprons a startling contrast to the iridescent sheen of the rest of their bodies. They lumbered heavily in the branches, and I was suddenly aware of Reilly sleeping on the sofa. This was too good a sight for him to miss.

"Come and have a look at this, Reilly," I coaxed.

He was lounging comfortably and strategically among the folds of a crocheted rug and his old favourite - my well-worn fluffy black jumper.

"I'm too tired."

"Oh come on, you'll be sorry you missed them!"

"Don't care. Another day I'll have a look."

"Yes, but they mightn't be there, then. You can't expect them to hang around for *you*."

"Don't care. I can't be bothered. Can't a cat get some sleep when he needs it?"

"You can go back to sleep later," I said firmly, scooping him into my arms and whispering to him as I took him to the kitchen window.

He spied the big birds but the viewpoint wasn't that good so I quietly went out the back door. Reilly went rigid in my arms when the birds lumbered to the lower branches, as if teasing the big fluffy cat who was now staring wide-eyed at them.

He gave a brief chatter and I moved up to the tree. Showing no inclination to climb into the fork of it, he then sank back into my shoulder and yawned. Both he and I knew it was hopeless trying to catch the birds, but it certainly wasn't my intention for him to try anyway. I simply felt as Reilly, due to boredom, had been getting into a fair bit of mischief over the previous few days, that a bit of excitement would do him good. Besides, it was a rare chance for me to see the magnificent *kereru* up close.

**

My friend and former neighbour Eileen visited. She lived a short distance down the street from where I had lived prior to going to Motueka. It was wonderful to see her again.

"Have you still got that dreadful cat?" she asked with a grin.

With a smile I said yes and asked her if she'd like to meet my other cat, Katie O'Brien. Eileen was enchanted with friendly little Katie and after an hour or so of 'catch-up' over tea and biscuits, when Eileen was ready to leave, I walked to the dairy with her and back around the block. It was a most pleasant time.

I returned the visit a few weeks later when the bulk of my work was done, and finally, some eight months after she had offered me a cup of tea on the day I was to leave Carter's Beach, I was able at last, to take Eileen up on her offer.

**

For the past year Reilly was sure he was too big to get underneath my bed. It suited Katie for him to think that way. Under my bed was the first place she headed for when Reilly was in one of his bullying moods.

The day we had a big thunderstorm was the day Reilly discovered he could indeed get under the new bed. That proves you can do anything you want to, providing there is incentive enough!

By flattening himself, rug-like, Reilly squeezed under and stayed there during the course of the storm. His discovery didn't faze Katie too much, however. She knew that even though Reilly could indeed get under the bed, his size meant that he was very limited in movement.

There were only two other things I knew of that made him nervous - the vacuum cleaner and the sound of an aerosol spray, whether it was for air freshener, perfume or whatever. The 'pock' sound of the lid coming off was enough to send Reilly leaping for the door. As far as he was concerned, *any* 'pock' sounds constituted the lid coming off a can of flea spray.

And being sprayed for fleas is something he simply would not tolerate. Flea collars worked for a while, but he would find some way of slipping them off, even herbal ones. But one had to persevere, and I'd had a lot of practice.

Despite the similar sound of the lid coming off a can of whipped cream, Reilly knew the difference and would come running for his treat. It was reminiscent of the day of his birthday anniversary, when he had the ultimate treat of whipped cream over top of a raw mince 'cake'.

"Gimme, gimme, woman!"

"I'm giving you, I'm giving you...."

"But not soon enough...oh yum yum. That's *very* nice!"

"Satisfied?"

"Yeah, until next time!"

He gazed at me with whipped cream clinging to his whiskers. Somehow on Reilly, the sight did not demean him in any way. If anything, it added a certain kind of panache to his already striking face.

**

The days gradually grew warmer, interspersed with the occasional bitterly cold day or two which was a stern reminder that although it was spring, winter wasn't finished with, not by a long shot!

The big eucalyptus tree at the front of the property constantly dropped its heavy leaves which rattled when the spring wind teased them over the concrete patio in front of the small cottage I was renting.

Sometimes the rattling leaves had a desolate sound that found an echo within me. Those sudden, sad moods were immediately dispersed with when Katie squealed for attention. That particular squeal meant she had brought me a leaf or twig - or even a piece of eucalyptus bark - for my attention. Reilly would look on with a gleam in his eye.

"Huh. What a fuss to gain your attention. All *I* gotta do is stand on my hind legs, lean against the door and stare in."

"*Not* so smart!" I exclaimed with relish. "You shouldn't have *told* me!"

Reilly looked at me with those incredible gold eyes half closed, a smirk hovering. Of course! I suddenly realized what that smirk was for. It didn't matter whether or not I had realized what Reilly's ploy was. The point was that I knew I would still be unable to resist him. And even if I *did* resist him for a while, there is something distinctly unnerving about a cat's determined stare. Turn one's back, and you can still feel the stare. It invades every part of one's consciousness and no matter what form it takes, the result - a mixture of exasperation and compassion pulling at the heartstrings - has that door opened. And the cat enters with a meow and a chirrup, as much to say: "what took you so long? But I forgive you, even though can't you see I'm starving?"

Reilly sometimes accompanied his stare by lifting his two front paws to rest them on the lower panel of the French door. With just his head and paws visible over the door panel, and with his prolonged stare, the effect was most unnerving: a sort of cat version of Kilroy wuz here.

**

CHAPTER THIRTEEN

A Dreaming Time

Reilly was back in one of his favourite spots - lying on the sofa on my old black fluffy jumper. He was asleep and dreaming, his first bad dream in a long while. He snored, growled and hissed, then suddenly sat up and blinked at me owlishly.

"It was a bad dream, Reilly. What were you dreaming about?"

"How should *I* know? I was asleep until a hissing cat woke me up."

"That was *you*, cat."

"I should know whether I'm hissing or not, woman."

"Well, this time you didn't know. Some dream you had! Maybe you'd better not go back to sleep!"

"Are you bossing me around?"

"Would I do that?" I asked innocently.

"*Would* I! *Would* I! No indeed, if you say not."

He yawned, looked at me sleepily, and promptly dozed off again, the bad dream erased from his memory.

**

I was not well, having had one extended bout of 'flu and then, like every second person in the district, I succumbed to a second, and worse dose of the 'flu which lasted for two months. One Sunday when I was feeling particularly lethargic I did my exercises in an attempt to ease the lethargy. It didn't work. I sat on the sofa next to Reilly and had a sudden coughing fit. Reilly opened one eye and then the other and *stared.*

"*Must* you do that?"

"I can't help it Reilly."

"Take something for it."

"I have; nothing seems to work."

I had another coughing fit and Reilly got up (I could almost hear his long-suffering sigh) and moved to the other end of the sofa and positively glared at me.

"You interrupted a good sleep, woman!"

"Selfish beast! If *you* were coughing, I'd be really worried about you, but do *you* care when I'm not feeling well? No, you do not!"

"If you think you already know the answer, why ask *me?*"

"Not only sarcastic, but cold and heartless as well."

"I'm an independent, tough tomcat."

"Sure, but who looks after *you* when you're sick?"

"I've never been sick!"

"What if you were?"

"What if! What if! Who do you suppose? *You*, woman! *You're* supposed to attend to my needs!"

"And little thanks I get, if any!" I complained.

His eyes narrowed and he yawned.

"You should consider it a privilege and not think about being thanked. It isn't necessary."

"Huh!" I said, affronted. "What about the time you were quite sick and could hardly jump up onto the sofa?"

"What about it?"

"Do you remember how I carefully cuddled you and prayed for you, and also asked my friend Wendy to pray for you?"

"Of course I remember! But did you take me to the vet? No, you did not! I could have been a dying cat!"

I eyed him grimly. "But you weren't though, were you?"

"I could have been!"

"Not after the prayers we said right away! And, you picked up right away. Anyway, you know you don't like going to the vet."

"A necessary evil, although I do concede that one or two of those animal doctors are quite nice. It's when they stick that glass thing up my rear that I have this terrible desire to do something equally horrible and undignified to them!"

"Such as what?"

"Such as...oh, let me think for a moment."

He paused and shut his eyes. I thought it was a ploy to go back to sleep but then he opened his eyes again.

"Apart from chewing their fingers in the best way I know how, which as you know is pretty drastic and fierce of me, I think they deserve to be urinated on. Oh yes, I like that idea...far better than spitting at them even. It's a good way to show my utter contempt, and at the same time I can relieve myself, of course. We cats are very good at that, and the more pungent, the better!"

"That's not very nice, Reilly," I said, fighting off another coughing fit.

"And nor is what they do to me!"

"It's for your own good...."

"For your own good! For your own good!" he mimicked. "If someone stuck a glass thing up your rear and said: 'it's for your own good,' would you believe them?"

"As long it was a doctor or nurse, I trusted them and there were good reasons for the check on my temperature...that's what the glass thing is, after all...a thermometer, you daft cat....well, I wouldn't mind, I suppose! Anyway, it's mostly put in one's mouth."

"Hopefully not directly after being up one's rear," he snickered.

"Don't be crude. Certainly not!"

"I don't think I'll understand you humans' weird way of thinking...no, not in a million *years!*"

"I'm tired of this conversation, cat," I said, yawning.

Reilly simply closed his eyes and dismissed me - just like that! I felt like throwing a cushion at him but decided against it. At least these days while he was asleep, he was quiet. In earlier days, apart from his fairly regular choking spasms, he had nightmares.

His legs and paws would twitch, his face go into spasms and he would utter odd little cries. One afternoon during the course of a bad dream he flung himself off the sofa and looked dazed. Then stared suspiciously at me as if it was *my* fault!

That last bad dream was almost a surprise; it had been so long since he'd experienced one. All the same, I couldn't rule out the fact that it could happen again any day. So I suppose that yes, I should be grateful that he was quietly asleep, even though I was piqued at his dismissal of me.

And I *still* felt miserable. The 'flu had left me with a temporary loss of a sense of smell and taste, and I was also quite deaf. I turned on my small CD player; the volume was too low for me to hear while I worked. I turned it up a bit more and wondered why Reilly, who was trying to sleep, summoned up a glare that was supposed to stop me in my tracks. It didn't, of course. I didn't think I had done anything to earn his displeasure.

It wasn't until the next day that I realized how deaf I had been. I switched on the CD player and the band Herbs blasted forth into the crisp morning air. No wonder Reilly had glared at me so horribly the day before.

I remembered my most recent trip to Motueka and Nelson, while I still had the 'flu. *Good Heavens*, I'd thought, *those new tyres are marvellous! They've really cut back the road noise.*

Then I realized that I could hardly hear my car stereo either. How I was going to manage taking notes for stories, I didn't know. All the same, I managed, albeit with apologies and explanations when I had to ask interviewees to repeat what they had just said.

At least they were patient with me, which is more than I could say for Reilly. However, loud music is not conducive to a good sleep, so maybe Reilly did have something to complain about.

**

CHAPTER FOURTEEN

A Good Understanding

Still, after all the scratches, scrapes, bites, glares and backchat, I think Reilly and I have come to a pretty good understanding. The other day when I asked him if he'd like a walk to the beach he chirruped and seemed just like any other happy cat. It gave me a warm feeling as we walked, even though the words 'he's no ordinary cat' kept prodding my consciousness.

Reilly loved to run in the kerbing. It was as if he had his own little racetrack.

"And here comes Seamus O'Reilly, out in front - so far out in front there's no contest! Let's hear it for the cat, Seamus O'Reilly! O'Reilly for number one!"

"Really, cat, you're so conceited," I said amiably.

"If I don't love me, who else will?"

"Ha ha! You said a mouthful, cat," I puffed, trying to keep up with him.

"Easy to see *you're* out of condition."

"I prefer to keep my womanly curves."

"Curves! *Curves?"*

He stopped to look me up and down, and then he smirked.

"Well, if you say so, woman."

"Don't be rude. Carry on with your running!"

"Yeah, O'Reilly for number one! Fastest cat this side of the black stump!"

**

It was a mellow evening a few nights later. Feeling the need for a brisk walk, I asked Reilly if he'd like to come with me.

"Of course I would! Haven't you learned *anything* about me yet?"

"I've learned what a disrespectful cat you are," I said sourly.

"Yeah well."

"Yeah well yourself."

A familiar car pulled up on the opposite side of the road.

"I had a feeling it was you," my friend Ray said, chuckling. "I don't know anyone else who takes their cat for a walk!"

I laughed. "I'm also teaching Katie to come with us occasionally. She's discovering how much she enjoys it."

"Where is she?"

"At home. She didn't feel like going out with us this time."

I picked up Reilly who was alert to the night sounds. He began to growl and stare fixedly at the stone fence across the road. Both Ray and I looked to see what Reilly was growling at. It was a cat he'd had a 'little altercation' with on a couple of excursions to the beach.

Ray was amused when I told him that if a stranger came to the door, Reilly would growl like a dog.

"Nothing would surprise me about that cat!" Ray laughed. He told me that he'd heard on the grapevine, stories about my cat that would make one's hair curl. I commented that it hadn't worked on *him!* "I don't frighten easily!"

He drove on with a wave and a smile and Reilly and I completed our most pleasant walk around the block, made all the nicer by seeing Ray, who is a very kindly and humorous person.

**

One mild spring evening I went out the back door and my cats were there; Katie on the path and Reilly neatly curled around the clothesline on the small concrete pad at the base. He looked so endearing I simply had to pick him up. He struggled to get down and when I lowered him back down, he promptly curled up around the clothesline again.

What secrets did that clothesline hold? What vibrations could he feel through the strong pipe support? Or was he regressing to a previous century and maintaining a vigil around a symbolic flagpole?

Ah well, whatever secrets he had, he was not going to share those particular ones with me. It didn't matter. It was enough to see him curled up in that spot. I would never cease to be amazed at the little surprises he sprang on me.

On this particular day Reilly actually seemed to like me. Was there a catch? Was he mellowing or had he come to the conclusion that humans aren't so bad after all?

One never knew with Reilly.

"I will never surrender! I will never mellow! I shall fight on the shores...."

"You've already done that!" I interrupted, remembering the friendly spotted dog who, whimpering, took off at great speed following Reilly's onslaught.

"Don't interrupt, woman. I.....where was I?"

"In the trenches," I smirked, thinking of how he loved to run in the kerbing.

"I hadn't got that far. I'll start again. I will never surrender! I will never mellow! I shall fight on the shores and in the trenches...."

"You've done *that* too!" I interrupted yet again, this time remembering his skirmishes at the road edge with Misty from next door.

"Must you ruin a good speech?"

I bowed deeply. "Please accept my most humble apologies," I said with a grin.

Reilly looked at me suspiciously, but then he decided to relax and accept my apology.

"Yeah, well. I'm off for a drink."

"Where?"

"The toilet."

"That is not really acceptable."

"Just you watch me, woman!"

I followed him into the bathroom where he promptly leaped onto the toilet seat and poked his head down the bowl to drink. His plump fluffy rear and tail hung hilariously over the side. I chuckled. He brought his head up and peered around at me.

"It's elementary my dear woman. Toilet water is so much more acceptable than any old stuff out of a plastic bowl!"

I smiled. "Quite right, too, cat, if you say so." Although privately I thought differently.

He appeared mollified.

We had come a long way. My prayers had been answered tenfold.

Many times I've looked back and thought of how my prayers were answered. *God sure doesn't do things by halves,* I've often thought.

Reilly more than kept unwanted dogs off the property. He broadened and heightened my life.

And that's sure got to be God's Work.

**

ABOUT THE AUTHOR

Amber Jo Illsley is a former freelance journalist who lives in New Zealand's South Island. She recently gave up journalism after 12 years, because she didn't find it creative enough, to concentrate on the completion of several novels and beginning new novels. All have ripples of humour prancing through them. A keen supporter of the rights for animals, the author enjoys all of God's creatures - but especially cats.

Now living in Invercargill, one of the world's southernmost cities, the author is a country girl at heart and is living in the city, as she puts it: 'only as a means to an end'.